CALICO JOE

CALICO JOE

John Grisham

DOUBLEDAY LARGE PRINT HOME LIBRARY EDITION

Doubleday

New York London Toronto Sydney Auckland

This Large Print Edition, prepared especially for Doubleday Large Print Home Library, contains the complete, unabridged text of the original Publisher's Edition.

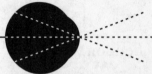

This Large Print Book carries the
Seal of Approval of N.A.V.H.

CALICO JOE

1

The tumor in my father's pancreas was removed last week in an operation that lasted five hours and was more difficult than his surgeons had expected. Afterward, they delivered the grim news that most people in his condition could not expect to live for more than ninety days. Since I knew nothing of the surgery, or the tumor, I was not there when he was given his death sentence. Communication is not a priority with my father. Ten years ago he divorced one wife and had found another before word filtered down to me.

His current wife—she's either number five or number six—eventually called and, after reintroducing herself, passed along the barest of details about the tumor and its related issues. Agnes explained that my father was not feeling well and didn't want to talk. I replied that he had never wanted to talk, regardless of how he felt. She asked me to spread the news to the rest of the family. I almost asked "Why?" but didn't want to bicker with this poor woman.

The rest of the family consists of my younger sister, Jill, and my mother. Jill lives in Seattle and, as far as I know, has not spoken to our father in at least ten years. She has two small children who have never met him, and never will. My mother, after surviving twelve years of marriage, got lucky and got out, taking Jill and me with her, and I have a hunch that the news of his impending death will have zero impact on her.

Needless to say, we do not get together at Christmas and exchange gifts by the fire.

After the phone call from Agnes, I sit at my desk and ponder life without Warren, my father. I started calling him Warren when I was in college because he was more of a person, a stranger, than a father. He did not object. He has never cared what I call him, and I have always assumed he prefers that I don't call him at all. At least I make the occasional effort; he never has.

After a few minutes, I admit the truth— life without Warren will be the same as life with him.

I call Jill and break the news. Her first question is whether I plan to attend the funeral, which is somewhat premature. She wants to know if she should try to visit him, to say hello and good-bye and go through the phony motions of acting as though she cares, when in fact she does not. Nor do I, and we both admit this. We have no love for Warren because he never cared for us. He abandoned the family when we were kids and has spent the past thirty years acting as though we do not exist. Jill and I are both parents now, and we find it inconceivable that a father can have no use for his own children.

"I'm not going," she finally declares. "Now, or later. How about you?"

"I don't know," I reply. "I'll have to think about it."

The truth is that I know I will go see him. He has burned most of the bridges in his life, but there is one rather substantial piece of unfinished business that he has to deal with before he dies.

My mother lives in Tulsa with her second husband. In high school, Warren was the superjock, and she was the homecoming queen, the most popular girl. Their wedding thrilled their small town, but after a couple of years with Warren all thrills were gone. I know they have not spoken to each other in decades, and why should they?

"Mom, I have some bad news," I say into the phone, trying to seem sufficiently somber.

"What is it?" she asks quickly, probably afraid it is one of her grandchildren.

"Warren's sick. Pancreatic cancer, he has less than three months to live."

A pause, relief, then, "I was assuming he was already dead."

And there you have it. His memorial service will not be packed with grieving family members.

"I'm sorry," she says, but she is not. "I guess you'll have to deal with it."

"I suppose."

"I don't want to be bothered with it, Paul, just call me when it's over. Or don't. I don't care what happens to Warren."

"I understand, Mom."

I know he hit her a few times, probably a lot more than I realized. And he drank and chased women and lived the hard life of a professional baseball player. He was arrogant and cocky, and from the age of fifteen he was accustomed to getting whatever he wanted because he, Warren Tracey, could throw a baseball through a brick wall.

We manage to move the conversation to the kids and when she might see them again. Because of her beauty and brains, she landed on her feet after Warren. She married a slightly older man, an executive for a drilling company, and he provided a fine home for Jill and me. He loves my mom, and that's all that matters.

I doubt if Warren ever did.

2

In the summer of 1973, the country was slowly emerging from the trauma of Vietnam. Spiro Agnew was in trouble and would eventually go down. Watergate was getting hot with much more to come. I was eleven years old and slightly aware of what was happening out there in the real world, but I was wonderfully unburdened by it. Baseball was my world, and little else mattered. My father pitched for the New York Mets, and I lived and died with each game. I pitched too, for the Scrappers in the White Plains Little League, and because my father

was who he was, great things were expected of me. I rarely met those expec-
tations, but there were moments of
promise.

By early July, the pennant race in the
National League East had settled into a
bland contest. All six teams—Mets, Pirates, Cardinals, Phillies, Cubs, and Ex-
pos—were hovering around .500 and
showing little enthusiasm for making a
run. In the West, the Reds and the Dodgers were pulling away. In the American
League, the Oakland A's, with their
swagger and colorful uniforms and long
hair, were looking to repeat their cham-
pionship of 1972.

My buddies and I followed the game
religiously. We knew each player and
every statistic. We checked every box
score, then replayed the games on the
sandlots of White Plains. Life at home
was not always pleasant, and my es-
cape was on the field. Baseball was my
best friend, and in mid-July 1973 the
game was about to be electrified like
never before.

It began quietly enough with a pulled hamstring. The first baseman for the Cubs AAA affiliate in Wichita went down as he rounded third and headed for home. The next day, Jim Hickman, the first baseman for the Cubs, injured his back. The team suddenly needed someone to play first, so they reached down to their AA club in Midland, Texas, and called up a twenty-one-year-old named Joe Castle. At the time, Castle was hitting .395 with twenty home runs, fifty RBIs, forty stolen bases, and only one error at first base. He was the hottest player in AA and was creating a buzz.

As the story goes, Castle was asleep in the cheap apartment he shared with four other minor leaguers when the call came from Chicago. An assistant coach drove him to the airport in Midland, and he caught a flight to Houston, where he waited two hours for a flight to Philadelphia. While he waited, he called his family in Arkansas with the thrilling news. When he arrived in Philadelphia, a cab delivered him to Veterans Stadium, where he was quickly fitted for a uniform, given Number 42, and hustled onto the field. The Cubs were already taking batting practice. Understandably, he was nervous, thrilled, almost bewildered, and when the manager, Whitey Lockman, said, "Get loose. You're starting at first and hitting seventh," Castle had trouble gripping his brand-new bat. In his first round of major-league batting practice, he swung at the first two pitches and missed.

He would not miss again for a long time.

In the dugout before the game, he huddled with Don Kessinger, the Cubs veteran shortstop and another Arkansas boy. Kessinger had been an all-American in baseball and basketball at Ole Miss and was outgoing and laid back. He managed to keep the kid loose. His only advice was "Go up there swinging." The Cubs center fielder was Rick Monday, another veteran who had been born in Batesville, Arkansas, just down the White River from Joe's hometown. Between Kessinger and Monday, Joe managed to survive the worst case of pre-game jitters a player could imagine.

It was Thursday, July 12, a day base-ball would remember for a long time.

The Phillies pitcher was a lefty, Benny Humphries, a wild fastballer who walked as many as he struck out. As Joe strolled to the plate in the second inning, he grit-ted his teeth and again told himself to swing at the first pitch, wherever it hap-pened to be. Humphries thought the rookie should get introduced to major-league heat and unloaded everything he had. Joe, from the right side, guessed fastball, made perfect contact, and hit a shot that landed twenty rows back in left center field. He sprinted around the bases, much too excited for any kind of victory trot, and was in the dugout be-ing congratulated before he caught his breath.

He was not the first major leaguer to homer on the first pitch he saw. In fact, he was the eleventh. Forty-six homered in their first at bat, eleven on the first pitch. Nonetheless, his name was in the record book. It was now open, and Joe Castle wasn't finished with it.

In the fifth inning, Humphries started off with a fastball high and tight, a brushback meant as a warning, but Joe didn't get the message. He worked the count to 3 and 1, then yanked a fastball down the left field line, where it barely scraped the inside of the foul pole. The third base umpire was quick to twirl his right index finger signaling a home run. Joe, who was rounding first and following the ball, kicked into a sprint and slowed slightly as he neared home plate. Now a record belonged only to him and one other. In 1951, Bob Nieman of the St. Louis Browns homered in his first two major-league at bats.

The Mets were playing the Braves in Atlanta that night, and the game was not on television. I was in Tom Sabbatini's basement listening to Lindsey Nelson, the Mets' wonderful play-by-play announcer, who informed us of what had just happened in Philadelphia. It didn't take much to get Lindsey excited. "He tied a record, folks," he said. "Think of the thousands of young men who've played this game, and only two have homered in their first two at bats."

"I wonder if he can do it three times," added Ralph Kiner, the Hall of Fame slugger and Lindsey's sidekick.

The Cubs chased Humphries in the sixth, and the Phillies brought in a middle reliever, a right-hander named Tip Gallagher. When Joe left the on-deck circle in the top of the seventh, the score was tied 4–4, and the Phillies fans, always vocal, were silent. There was no applause, just curiosity. To their surprise, Joe dug in from the left side. Since there was no scouting report, the Phillies did not know he was a switch-hitter. No one had bothered to notice him during batting practice. He looked at a curveball low, then fouled off the next two fastballs. With two strikes, he shortened his stance and choked up three inches on the bat. The previous season, he led the Texas League with the lowest strike-out percentage of any hitter. Joe Castle was at his most dangerous with two strikes.

A slider missed low, then Gallagher came with a fastball away. Joe went with the pitch and slapped it hard to left center, a line drive that kept rising until it cleared the wall by five feet. As he circled the bases for the third consecutive time, he did so with a record that seemed untouchable. No rookie had ever homered in his first three at bats.

———

Joe Castle was from Calico Rock, Arkansas, a tiny, picturesque village on a bluff above the White River, on the eastern edge of the Ozark Mountains. It was Cardinals country, and had been since the days of Dizzy Dean, an Arkansas farm boy and leader of the infamous Gashouse Gang in the 1930s. His brother Paul, nicknamed Daffy, was also a pitcher on the same team. In 1934, at the height of the Gang's fame, Dizzy predicted in spring training that he and Daffy would combine for fifty wins. They won forty-nine—thirty for Dizzy and nineteen for Daffy. Twenty years later, Stan Musial, the greatest Cardinal of all, was revered to the point of being worshipped. With a radio on every front porch, the town, like countless others in the Midwest and the Deep South, fol-

lowed the beloved Cardinals with a pas-
sion during the long, hot summer nights.
KMOX out of St. Louis carried the games,
and the familiar voices of Harry Caray
and Jack Buck could be heard on every
street and in every car.

On July 12, though, the dials in Calico
Rock had been switched to WGN out of
Chicago, and Joe's friends and family
were hanging on every pitch. The Cardinals–Cubs rivalry was the greatest in
the National League, and though many
in Calico Rock found it difficult to believe they were rooting for the hated
Cubs, they were suddenly doing so, and
with a fervor. In a matter of hours, they
had been converted to Cubs fans. After
the first home run, a crowd quickly gathered outside Evans Drug Store on Main
Street. The second home run sent them
into a giddy celebration, and the crowd
continued to grow. When Joe's parents,
two brothers, their wives, and their small
children showed up to join the party,
they were greeted with bear hugs and
cheers.

The third home run sent the entire

town into orbit. They were also celebrat-
ing in the streets and pubs of Chicago.

———

As stunning as his first three at bats
had been, Joe's fourth would endear
him to baseball purists forever. Top of
the ninth, score tied 6–6, two outs, Don
Kessinger standing on third, a tough
right-hander named Ed Ramon on the
mound. As Joe stepped to the plate, a
few of the eighteen thousand fans
clapped politely, then an odd silence
settled across Veterans Stadium. Ramon's first pitch was a fastball on the
outside part of the plate. Joe waited,
then whipped his bat like a broomstick,
crushing the ball and lining it a few
inches outside the bag at first base, a
foul ball, but an impressive one nonetheless. Ernie Banks, the Cubs first base
coach, did not have time to react, and if
the ball had hit him, he would have been
seriously maimed. Willie Montanez, the
Phillies first baseman, moved to his left,
but only after the ball had caromed off
the stands and was rolling into right
field. Instinctively, Montanez took two

steps back. Joe noticed this and changed his plans. The second pitch was a changeup, high. With the count 1 and 1, Ramon tried another fastball. As soon as he released it, Joe hesitated a split second, then broke for first base with his bat trailing. It tapped the ball slightly and sent it dribbling toward the second baseman, Denny Doyle, who was as startled as Ramon, Montanez, and everyone else in the stadium. By the time Doyle got to the ball, or the ball got to Doyle, Joe was ten feet past first base and slowing down along the right field foul line. Kessinger walked home with the eventual winning run. The crowd sat in stunned silence. Players from both teams looked on in disbelief. With a chance to hit four home runs in a game— a feat baseball had seen only nine times in a hundred years—the kid chose instead to lay down a perfect drag bunt to score the go-ahead run.

———

Most of those listening to the game along Main Street in Calico Rock had seen the identical drag bunt, though Joe

Castle had seldom needed it. They had seen far more tape-measure shots and inside-the-park home runs. His oldest brother, Charlie, who was sitting on a bench outside the drugstore, had taught him the drag bunt when he was ten years old. He'd also taught him to switch-hit, steal bases, and foul off pitches that were close but not what he wanted. The middle brother, Red, had hit him a million ground balls and perfected his footwork at first base. Both brothers had taught him how to fight.

"Why'd he bunt?" someone in the crowd asked Charlie.

"To score the run and take the lead," Charlie replied. Plain and simple.

The Cubs announcers, Vince Lloyd and Lou Boudreau, had been plowing through the record book during the game and were certain that they had their facts straight. Three home runs in the first game of a career was a first. Four consecutive hits in a first game tied a modern-day record, though some rookie had five hits back in 1894.

Chicago won 7–6, and by the time the game ended, virtually every Cubs fan was tuned in. History had been made, and they didn't want to miss it. Lou Boudreau promised his listeners that he would soon have Joe wired up for a postgame interview.

The crowd in Calico Rock continued to grow, and the mood was rowdy, the pride palpable. A half hour after the game was over, Lou Boudreau's voice came across the radio with "I'm in the visitors' locker room with Joe Castle, who, as you might guess, is surrounded by reporters. Here he is."

Sudden silence on Main Street in Calico Rock; no one moved or spoke.

"Joe, not a bad first game. What are you thinking right now?"

"Well, I would like to say hello to my family and friends back home in Calico Rock. I wish you could be here. I still can't believe it."

"Joe, what were you thinking when you stepped to the plate in the second inning?"

"I was thinking fastball and I was swinging at the first pitch. Got lucky, I guess."

"No player has ever homered in his first three at bats. You're in the record book."

"I guess. I'm just happy to be here. This time last night I was playing in Midland, Texas. Still hard to believe."

"Indeed it is. I gotta ask you—and I know you've already been hit with this—but what were you thinking in the ninth inning? You had a chance to hit four home runs in a game, yet you bunted."

"I was thinking about one thing—getting Don home from third for the go-ahead run. I love playing baseball, but it's no fun if you're not winning."

"Well, you got a nice little streak going here. Think you can keep it up tomorrow night?"

"I haven't thought about tomorrow night. Don and some of the guys are taking me out for a steak, and I'm sure we'll discuss it then."

"Good luck."

"Yes sir. Thank you."

Few in Calico Rock went to bed before midnight.

———

As promised, my mother awakened me at 6:00 a.m. so I could watch the early morning New York news programs. I was hoping for a glimpse of Joe Castle. Channel 4 did a quick rundown on the National League games. The Mets had won in Atlanta to put them two games over .500. Then there was Joe Castle sprinting around the bases in Philadelphia, once, twice, three times. The drag bunt, though, got as much airtime as the three home runs. The guy could fly.

My mother brought in the *New York Times* from the driveway. On the front page of the sports section was a black-and-white photo of Joe Castle and a long story about his historic debut. I found the scissors, cut it out, and started a new scrapbook, one of many I meticulously maintained. When the Mets were in town and my father was home, I was forced to save the newspapers for a few days before clipping the baseball stories.

I loved it when the Mets were on the road. My father was gone, and our house was peaceful and pleasant. When he was around, though, the mood was far different. He was a self-absorbed, brooding man with seldom a kind word for any of us. He had never met his potential, and this was always the fault of someone else—the manager, his teammates, the owners, even the umpires. On the nights after he pitched, he often came home late and drunk, and that's when the trouble started. I suspected, even at the age of eleven, that my parents would not stay together.

He rarely called home when the Mets were away. I often thought how wonderful it would be for my father to check in after a game and talk baseball with me. I watched or listened to every Mets game and had a dozen questions, but I guess he was too busy going out with the boys.

For me, baseball was a joy to play when my father wasn't watching. Because of his schedule, he rarely had the chance to see my games, and that was an indescribable relief. When he was there, though, I had no desire to play. He would lecture me on the way to the park, snarl at me during the game, and,

worst of all, berate me all the way home.
He even slapped me once as soon as
we were driving away from the field.
From the age of seven, I cried after every game my father saw me play.

3

Sara and I met during our sophomore years at the University of Oklahoma. We married a month after we graduated. Warren was invited to both the commencement exercises and the wedding but failed to show. This surprised no one.

We have three beautiful daughters and live in Santa Fe, where I write software for an aerospace firm. Sara was an interior designer until the girls came along and she decided to become a full-time mother. Not surprisingly, I was thrilled with each birth, each healthy baby, and not the least disappointed in the gender God selected for us. I did not want a boy, because I did not want to see him pick up a baseball and start tossing it around. Most of my friends have a boy or two, and they have all coached the game at some level. I am sure I would have felt the temptation to do likewise with a boy, so I am relieved to have all girls.

I quit the game when I was eleven years old and haven't watched an inning in thirty years.

My employer is one of those progressive companies with all manner of benefits and flexible work rules. I could practically work from home, but I enjoy the office, my colleagues, even my bosses. It's exciting to watch the technology spring to life, evolve, and eventually hit the market.

I explain to my boss that I need a few days off for a quick trip unrelated to my job. He says fine. I tell Sara my plans, and she understands completely. She knows the history, and I guess we both have known this trip would one day become inevitable.

I drive to the airport in Santa Fe and buy a one-way ticket to Memphis.

———

When Warren was thirty-five years old, he managed to persuade an old friend in the Orioles organization to give him one final tryout in spring training. He could still throw hard, but he had no control; plus, his name was toxic, and no other team would touch him. He bombed in his first appearance and was cut the next day. He called home and informed my mother he planned to stay in Florida, where, supposedly, some minor-league team wanted him as a pitching coach. This was not true and I knew it. I was twelve by then and well aware that my father was a habitual liar. A few months later she filed for divorce, and when the school year ended, we moved to Hagerstown, Maryland, to live with her parents.

Warren Tracey retired from the game with a record of sixty-four wins and eighty-four losses, a career earned run average of 5.85. In sixteen seasons, he played for the Pirates, Giants, Indians,

Royals, Astros, and Mets, and spent more time in the minors than in the majors. His three-year stint with the Mets was his longest stay anywhere, and they sent him down to AAA at least four times. He struck out 430 batters and walked 416. His name is in the record book only because he led the league in hit batsmen in 1972. He was never happy anywhere, and when he wasn't being traded, he was demanding to be traded. Not a particularly stellar career, but baseball fans know that only one player out of ten who signs a minor-league contract makes it to the Bigs for a single game. When I was very young and still impressionable, I was proud of the fact that my father was a major leaguer. No other kid on my street could make that claim. As I grew older, though, I often wished I had a normal dad, one who enjoyed having a catch in the backyard and coaching his son.

When he was with the Mets, he left for spring training each year in early January, long before he was supposed to report. He used various excuses for this, but the reality was that he wanted to get away from home, to play golf every day, to work on his tan, and to drink and catch up with old girlfriends. Jill and I didn't care which excuse he used. We were relieved to have him back on the road.

After the year in Hagerstown, my mother informed us that he had remarried down in Florida. Jill and I thought this was terrible news because he and his new wife might decide to start a family.

On the leg from Dallas to Memphis, I open my old scrapbook on Joe Castle. It is filled with newspaper clippings, magazine articles, the August 6 edition of *Sports Illustrated*, with Joe on the cover, and the item I had treasured most during that remarkable summer of 1973, an eight-by-ten black-and-white photo of his youthful, smiling face. Across the bottom he had printed neatly, "To Paul Tracey, with best wishes," then scribbled his autograph. I had a whole collection of these when I was a boy. My buddies and I wrote letters to hundreds of professional players, asking for autographed photos. Occasionally one responded, and to get a photo in the mail was a reason to strut. My father got a few of these letters but was too important to grant a favor. He constantly griped about the fans who wanted autographs.

I hid my scrapbooks from my father. In his twisted opinion, he was the only player worthy of my adulation.

After I quit the game, my mother secretly stored my memorabilia in the attic. She gave it back—two cardboard boxes full—after I got married. At first I wanted to burn it, but Sara intervened, and it survives until this day.

I have never been in Memphis in August, and when I step out of the airport terminal, I have trouble breathing. The air is hot and sticky, and my shirt is wet within minutes. I ride a shuttle to Avis, get my rental car, crank up the AC, and head west, across the Mississippi River, into the flat farmlands of the Arkansas delta.

Calico Rock is four hours away.

4

On Friday, July 13, 1973, the front page of the sports section of the *Chicago Tribune* ran the bold headline "Four for Four." There was a large black-and-white photo of Joe Castle, and three different stories about his historic first game. The entire city was buzzing about "the kid." For a tribe hardened by years of frustration, Cubs fans had a rare moment to gloat.

Joe slept late in his hotel room, called his parents collect and talked for an hour with them and his brothers, then had a long, late breakfast with Don Kessinger and Rick Monday. He killed some more time by calling his teammates in Midland. Reporters were looking for him, but he was already tired of their attention. At 4:00 p.m., he stepped onto the team bus for the quick ride back to Veterans Stadium. In the locker room, Whitey Lockman walked over and said, "You're batting third tonight, kid, don't screw it up." Two hours before game time, Joe walked onto the field, stretched and warmed up, then took one hundred ground balls at first base. It seemed as though time had stopped. He couldn't wait for game time.

When he stepped to the plate with two outs in the top of the first, there were forty-five thousand Phillies fans in the stadium. There were also millions of Cubs fans glued to TVs and radios. With the count at two balls, he ripped a double into the right field corner. Five for five. In the top of the third, with the bases loaded, he singled to right and drove in two. Six for six. In the fifth, with the bases empty, two outs, and the infield back, and from the right side, he pushed a bunt toward third. When Mike

Schmidt picked it up bare-handed, Joe was flying past first base, and there was no throw. Seven for seven. In the seventh inning, he bounced a fastball off the top of the scoreboard in left center field, and as he rounded the bases, at a somewhat slower pace, the Phillies fans offered subdued but prolonged applause.

Eight for eight.

With two outs in the top of the ninth, and the Cubs leading 12–2 in a blowout, Joe dug in from the left side. He had two singles, a double, and a home run, and many in the crowd and legions of those watching and listening were praying for a triple. Vince Lloyd and Lou Boudreau were openly begging for one on the radio. Hitting for the cycle—single, double, triple, home run—was a rare event in baseball. It happened, on average, three times each season, and since Joe seemed intent on crushing all records, why not hit for the cycle? Instead, he fouled off ten straight pitches, worked the count full, then hit one of the longest home runs in the history of Veterans Stadium. As he rounded third,

Mike Schmidt said, "Not a bad game, kid."

Nine for nine, with five home runs.

Unbridled mania swept the streets of the North Side of Chicago.

––––

After the Scrappers game, our last of the regular season, the team met for a party in Tom Sabbatini's backyard. Mr. Sabbatini had the grill going—hot dogs and cheeseburgers—and most of the parents were there, including my mother. My father was pitching that night in Atlanta, but we were not interested in that game. Instead, Mr. Sabbatini rigged up an impressive radio, and we listened to WCAU out of Philadelphia. It was not unusual in those days to scan the dial with a small transistor radio and pick up games from New York, Philadelphia, Boston, even Montreal and Baltimore. I often spent hours in my room at night keeping track of several games.

Each time Joe Castle stepped to the plate, the party came to a halt as we crowded closer to the radio. Harry Kalas was the Phillies announcer, and his

voice grew more excited as the game
went on, even though his team was getting drubbed. With each of Joe's hits,
and especially with the two home runs,
we yelled and jumped around as if we
were lifelong Cubs fans. At one point,
Harry said, "I suspect there are a lot of
Cubs fans out there tonight, especially
in the little town of Calico Rock, Arkansas."

When Joe came up in the ninth, we
were so nervous we were bouncing on
our tiptoes. After each foul ball, we took
a deep breath, then leaned in closer to
the radio. Harry said, "Two strikes on
Castle." We heard the crack of the bat,
and Harry, in his patented home-run
call, described what was happening:
"The pitch . . . there's a drive . . . this
ball is . . . outta here! In the upper
deck . . . Mike Schmidt territory . . . Greg
Luzinski territory. Five for five . . . Nine
for nine. Unbelievable, baseball fans,
simply unbelievable."

History was happening, and though
we were only eleven years old and far
away from the game, we felt as if we
were a part of it. We had already checked

the schedule and knew that it would be late August before the Cubs arrived at Shea Stadium. My buddies were already dropping hints about needing tickets.

After three games in Philadelphia, and ten for the road trip, the Cubs were going home. As Harry Kalas signed off, he said, "I cannot imagine the reception Joe Castle will get tomorrow afternoon at Wrigley Field. I wouldn't mind being there myself."

———

The Cubs left Philadelphia at midnight and arrived two hours later at O'Hare. As the team boarded a bus to leave the airport, Joe Castle got his first taste of fame. Several dozen Cubs fans were waiting behind a chain-link fence for a glimpse of their new star. He walked over, shook a few hands, thanked them for coming out at such an hour, then hustled back to the bus, where his teammates were waiting, eager to leave but also enjoying the moment. The front office arranged a hotel room under an alias, and Joe finally fell asleep at 3:00 a.m.

Not long afterward, his parents and two brothers left Calico Rock for the long drive to Chicago. The Cubs played the Giants at 2:00 p.m. Saturday, and only a sudden death would keep them away from Wrigley.

———

Cable television was still a few years in the future, and the only games televised nationally were the World Series, the All-Star Game, and the NBC Game of the Week on Saturday afternoon with Curt Gowdy and Tony Kubek. The July 14 game was scheduled to be televised from Tiger Stadium in Detroit, where the A's were in town. At dawn, NBC, along with the rest of the baseball world, awakened to the irresistible story of Joe Castle and his stunning debut in Philadelphia. Suddenly the biggest game of the day was the Cubs versus the Giants; indeed, no other game was even close. Every baseball fan in America would be itching for news out of Wrigley.

It was raining in Detroit, not a heavy rain, but moisture nonetheless, and at dawn NBC made the controversial and long-remembered decision to move the Game of the Week to Chicago. The Tigers and the A's squawked for a few weeks afterward, but no one listened. Joe Castle owned major-league baseball in July 1973, and NBC never regretted its decision. The gamble paid off; it was to be another historic game.

Curt Gowdy and Tony Kubek were roused from their sleep in Detroit and put on a plane to Chicago, where NBC was scrambling to piece together a production crew and get enough cameras wired up at Wrigley. The network was also praying for clear skies. By mid-morning, the weather was better in Detroit than in Chicago; indeed, when the Tigers game started at 2:00 p.m., there was not a cloud to be seen anywhere. Gowdy and Kubek would later admit that they were thrilled at the change of venue because of the excitement at Wrigley Field.

In 1957, Kubek, the Yankees longtime shortstop, played against one Walt Dropo, better known as Moose because he was six feet five and weighed 220 pounds. In 1950, Dropo was the American League Rookie of the Year, but injuries soon derailed a promising career. Over the next eleven seasons, Moose Dropo played for several American League teams and hit .270 with 152 home runs, respectable numbers but not the kind to be remembered. However, in July 1952, while playing for Detroit against the Yankees, he hit safely in twelve consecutive at bats, without a walk. It was an astonishing feat, a record regarded by many experts as unbreakable.

Suddenly Moose Dropo's forgotten career was attracting attention. The Saturday edition of the *Chicago Sun-Times* ran an old photo of Dropo alongside a new one of Joe Castle, and beneath them was the question in bold print: "Twelve In A Row?" The *Tribune* sports page blared: "Nine for Nine!"

Wrigley Field was built in 1914, and various expansions over the decades brought its capacity to 41,000. The previous season, 1972, the Cubs averaged 16,600 fans for each home game. Until the arrival of Joe Castle, the 1973 Cubs were averaging 16,800. By 10:00 a.m.

Saturday, crowds were gathering around the ticket booths at Wrigley. Long lines were forming along Addison Street. Parties were under way on the rooftops beyond left field. Wrigleyville was alive, and as the morning dragged on, it began to rock. Everyone was desperately looking for a ticket.

A Cubs equipment manager fetched Joe from his hotel and sneaked him into an unnoticed maintenance door under the right field bleachers. When Joe took his first step onto the turf at Wrigley, it was just after 11:00 a.m. He had slept less than three hours because sleep was all but impossible. The gates had been opened, and the stands were filling quickly. No one recognized him in his street clothes. Near the home dugout, he introduced himself to several of the groundskeepers and politely said no to a reporter. In the Cubs dressing room, he admired his new locker as he changed into his uniform. A light lunch was served, and Joe was eating a sandwich with Don Kessinger when a trainer said, "Hey, Joe, your parents are here."

In a narrow hallway outside the locker

room, Joe hugged his mother and em-
braced his father and brothers, Red and
Charlie. All five were in various stages of
disbelief, with Joe perhaps being the
most composed. "It's just baseball," he
said. "They'll get me out eventually."

Not surprisingly, Red had some advice. "Keep swinging. If it's close, don't
take a chance."

Charlie added, "You're gonna see
breakin' stuff. No more fastballs. Stay
back."

"Right, right," Joe said, laughing, then
took his family inside the locker room
for a quick tour. They were overwhelmed,
sleepwalking through an adventure they
had dreamed about for years.

———

The Giants came into Wrigley five
games behind the Dodgers in the West.
Willie Mays was gone; in fact, he was
idling away his waning days with the
Mets. But the Giants still had Willie Mc-
Covey and Bobby Bonds, and their record was slightly better than the Cubs'
on July 14. Their starter was Ray Hiller,

a left-hander with six wins and seven losses.

There were at least forty-one thousand rowdy Cubs fans packed into Wrigley at 2:00 p.m. Countless others watched from the rooftops beyond the left field wall. When Joe Castle's name was called in the bottom of the first, a deafening ovation shook the old place and buried the voices of Curt Gowdy and Tony Kubek.

Hiller was a junk dealer whose fastball rarely topped eighty. He lobbed up a couple of harmless curveballs, and Joe resisted the urge to flail away. His third pitch was some knuckle-curve combo that fluttered high and outside, and with the count 3 and 0, Joe got the signal to hit away. Hiller came in with a slider that didn't move much, and Joe swung with a vengeance. The ball lifted high and lazy at first, then it seemed to gain speed. Soon, there was no doubt it was gone; the question was, where would it land? Gary Matthews, the left fielder, took two steps back, then stopped, turned around, put his hands on his hips, and watched to see where it was going. The ball eventually bounced off the fifth-floor facade of a building, some 470 feet from home plate. Perhaps he was fatigued from all the home-run trots, or maybe he was learning to savor the moment, but whatever the reason, Joe rounded the bases at a slower pace, but not slow enough to aggravate the pitcher. "Never show up the pitcher," Red and Charlie had drilled into him since the age of ten.

Wrigley Field had never been louder. The standing ovation roared until Joe took a step out of the dugout, tipped his cap, and acknowledged the adoring crowd. Then he blew a kiss at his mother, who was in the owner's seats in the second row.

Ten for ten, with six home runs.

Joe led off in the bottom of the third with the score tied 1–1. On the first pitch, he faked a bunt, and the entire Giant infield reacted in spasms. Ed Goodson at third and Chris Speier at short were on their heels before the pitch, expecting a line shot from an astonishingly quick bat. They eventually shot forward. Tito Fuentes did the same, while Mc-

Covey stutter-stepped around first base. After Hiller recovered from the pitch, he bolted upright, as if terrified of a bunt. Evidently, the Giants scouts had been alerted to Joe's bunting skills. Ball one. Hiller kept his fastball off the center of the plate, opting instead to pick at the corners and hope for the best. His second pitch was a fastball, five inches outside. Joe waited and waited, then went with the pitch and slapped it to right field for a single.

Eleven for eleven.

It may have been the thrill of watching history in the making, or it could have been the clearing skies and sunshine and cold beer, or perhaps even the excitement that a full house always provided, or probably all of the above, but the atmosphere at Wrigley was electric. By now, Joe was receiving a standing ovation when he stepped into the on-deck circle, another when he stepped to the plate, and of course an even rowdier one with each hit.

He tipped his cap and helmet to the crowd, then took a lead off first.

His twelfth at bat came in the bottom

of the sixth with the Cubs up 3–2. When the forty-one thousand faithful stood to applaud, they remained standing. On television, Curt Gowdy admitted to having a knot in his stomach. On the radio, Vince Lloyd described it as the most dramatic moment he could remember. Lou Boudreau went silent.

Hiller had abandoned his fastball altogether and was surviving on long, looping curves, changeups, and a nasty combo of a slider and curve known as a slurve. Joe fouled off the first two pitches, both balls, and cursed himself for swinging at bad pitches. He shortened his stance, choked up, and took a ball high. The fourth pitch was a slow, dropping curve, a pitch that might cross the plate at the knees or six inches lower, and Joe took no chances. He chopped down on the pitch, and it slammed hard into home plate—a fair ball. It ricocheted high into the air toward third, where Goodson charged and waited, and waited. When he finally caught the ball, Joe was past first base for his twelfth consecutive hit. Move over Moose Dropo.

Again, he tipped his hat to the screaming crowd. Willie McCovey, a fierce com-
petitor, tapped him on the rear with his
glove and said, "Congratulations, kid."
Joe could only smile and nod. He was
dreaming and in another world. Not too
many years earlier, his baseball card
collection included a double "All-Star"
selection featuring both Willie McCovey
and Willie Mays.

In the top of the eighth, McCovey hit
a two-run bomb that sailed over the
right field bleachers and was probably
never found. The Giants led 5–3 when
the Cubs came to bat in the bottom of
the inning.

The score was one thing, but the ma-
jority of the fans were not there just to
watch a ball game. It was a rare moment to celebrate. Their beloved Cubs
had not won a World Series since 1908.
There had been some memorable moments—the 1945 team lost the Series in
seven games to Detroit—though this
had been during the "war years," when
the good players were serving in the
armed forces. There had been a few
Hall of Famers—Hack Wilson in the

1920s and Ernie Banks in the 1950s and 1960s. Generally speaking, though, Cubs fans were accustomed to disappointment. They were fiercely loyal, but also desperate for a team or a player that was better than the rest.

Joe's thirteenth at bat had enough pressure because of the first twelve hits, but add a runner at each base, two outs, and two runs down, and the tension on the field was suffocating. The crowd was standing, yelling, some were even praying. Hiller was gone, replaced by a right-hander named Bobby Lund, a veteran reliever who threw exceptionally hard. Joe would later admit that he preferred to hit from the left side because he could pick up the fastballs a bit quicker. He was always content to foul off pitches and work the count full, but in this, his thirteenth and possibly most important at bat in whatever career he might eventually have, he decided to be impatient. He took the first pitch, a high fastball, and after one look at Lund's delivery, he was ready. The second pitch was another fastball, maybe an inch outside, but close enough to rip. Joe hit a scorcher to right center, a bullet that Tito Fuentes at second actually leaped for and missed badly. The ball stayed ten feet off the ground until it crashed into the ivy, where Bobby Bonds played it on one hop and fired home. With two outs, the runners were off with contact, and Joe's double cleared the bases.

When he slid unchallenged into second base, he owned the record, the one that had been labeled "unbreakable." Standing on second, he put his hands on his knees and stared at the dirt and for a few seconds tried to believe and savor the moment. The stadium was manic; the noise was earsplitting.

The Giants catcher, Dave Rader, had the ball and, when the dust settled, called time. Slowly, he walked past the mound to second base, where he ceremoniously handed it to Joe Castle. The crowd roared even louder with this memorable act of sportsmanship.

Joe removed his helmet and acknowledged the adulation. The umpires were in no hurry to resume play. They were witnessing history, and the game is played without a clock. Finally, Joe

walked to the seats beside the Cubs
dugout and tossed the ball to his father.
Then he went back to second base and
put on his helmet. He looked deep into
center field and quickly wiped a tear
from his cheek. A camera caught it, and
Curt Gowdy and Tony Kubek made sure
the world saw that Joe Castle, standing
alone on second base and alone in the
record book, now a legend, was human
enough to show emotion.

5

After an hour on the flat, two-lane highways of northeastern Arkansas, I realize I am quite hungry. Outside the town of Parkin, I pull in to the gravel lot of a barbecue shack and hope for the best. To avoid potential conversation, I take a portion of my scrapbook to read during lunch. Over a pulled pork sandwich and a root beer, I flip through pages of press clippings I have not seen in decades.

As soon as Joe arrived in the majors, I began visiting the library in White Plains to collect stories from the Chicago newspapers. Using a massive Xerox machine near the periodicals section, I made copies at five cents each. The July 15 Sunday editions of both the *Sun-Times* and the *Tribune* were packed with stories and photos of Saturday's historic game. Joe was interviewed at length about the game, and it was obvious he was thoroughly enjoying the moment. Among many memorable quotes, he said such things as:

"Well, if they keep me in the lineup, I'll probably hit .750 for the season."

And, "Oh, sure, we have seventy-four games left. One home run per game is not out of the question."

And, "They'll get me out eventually."

And, "The pennant? That's already in the bag, man. We're thinking about the World Series. I want to play the A's."

In spite of these comments, it was clear he liked bantering with the press and much of what he said was tongue-in-cheek. The Chicago baseball reporters, a notoriously tough bunch, were in awe and described him as "cocky but not the least bit arrogant" and "at times obviously overwhelmed by what he had done." His teammates were stunned but also realistic. One said, "He'll cool off, but let's hope it takes a few weeks. Right now we've won four in a row, and that's all that matters." Whitey Lockman, when asked if Joe would remain in the lineup, retorted, "What, are you crazy?"

The postgame photos revealed a fresh-faced kid who looked all of twenty-one and was on top of the world. He was handsome, with deep-set blue eyes and curly, sandy hair, the kinds of looks that would soon attract women every-where he went. He was single and had no significant female in his life, accord-ing to one story.

Everyone was falling in love with Joe Castle.

———

I had watched the Game of the Week with my mother in our den and after-ward met Tom Sabbatini and Jamie Brooks at a sandlot where we tossed the ball around and talked nonstop about Joe. We took turns reenacting each of his at bats. On that glorious summer afternoon, there was no doubt that each of us would one day do something as dramatic as Joe Castle. We would play professional baseball, no question about that, the only unknown was for which team. Not surprisingly, the three of us decided that we would play for the Cubs, together, and for a long time.

I was having dinner with my mother and Jill when the phone rang. It was my coach, and he began by explaining that the All-Star voting had taken place that morning. I had been selected for the twelve-player roster, the only eleven-year-old to make the team. I was dreaming of this, of course, but I figured it was a long shot. I was stunned and elated, and after squealing this news to Mom and Jill, I wanted desperately to tell my father. But he was in Atlanta with the Mets, at the ballpark for a 7:00 p.m. game, and I knew he would not call afterward. Mom suggested I wait until late Sunday morning and call his hotel.

———

The sandwich is gone. I gather my scrapbook, pay the check, and continue my journey. Before long, I leave the rice and bean fields and enter hill country, then the Ozark Mountains, which are not really mountains but more like slightly larger hills. At Batesville, birthplace of Rick Monday, I cross the White River and follow it north, through Mountain View and into the Ozark National Forest. It is a beautiful drive along Highway 5, a narrow winding road that is probably worthy of a postcard in October, but it is August and the grass is brown.

As far as I could tell, Joe Castle still lives in Calico Rock. After his brief career ended, he returned home and dropped out of sight. There had been stories about him, but with time, and with virtually no access, the journalists and reporters had forgotten about him. One of the last efforts had been a visit by a writer for *Sports Illustrated* in 1977, but the town had quickly closed ranks, and almost no information was exchanged. The reporter could not find Joe and was asked to leave by his brother Red.

As I enter Calico Rock, I tell myself for the hundredth time that I am being foolish. Not only would I fail in my little mission, but there is also an element of danger.

It is a lovely village, on a bluff above the White River. Trout docks are bunched near the bridge; fishing is important along the river. I park in front of the shops on Main Street, and for a moment I wonder what it must have been like thirty years earlier when Joe's friends and family gathered in crowds to listen to Vince Lloyd and Lou Boudreau call the games during that magical summer. I can almost feel the heartbreak when Joe went down.

I am looking for a man named Clarence Rook, the owner of the *Calico Rock Record*, the small weekly newspaper that has been reporting the town's business for half a century. Mr. Rook has been with the paper for almost that long, and if he chooses not to cooperate, I really have no alternative plan. The office is on Main Street, three doors down from Evans Drug Store. I take a deep breath and walk inside. A young secretary in blue jeans greets me with a big smile and friendly hello.

"I'm looking for Mr. Clarence Rook," I say in a well-rehearsed line.

"He's pretty busy," she says, still smiling. "Can I help you?"

"No, but thanks. I really need to see him."

"Okay. Can I have a name?"

"Paul Casey. I'm a reporter with *Baseball Monthly*." These lies will not last long, but the truth simply will not work right now.

"Interesting," she says. "And what brings you to Calico Rock?"

"I'm working on a story," I reply, well aware of how vague I sound.

"Okay," she says, retreating. "Let me see what he's doing."

She disappears into the back. I can hear voices. The walls are lined with framed copies of old editions, and it doesn't take long to find one from July 1973. The bold headline read: "Joe Castle in Stunning Debut with Cubs." I take a step closer and begin reading. The story was written by Clarence Rook, as were most of the front-page articles, and it was filled with unabashed pride.

I have a copy of it in my scrapbook.

"Mr. Rook will see you," she reports, nodding to a narrow hallway. "First door on the right."

"Thanks," I say with a smile and head for the rear.

Clarence Rook is a colorful sight—red cheeks, white shirt, red bow tie, red suspenders, probably seventy years old, with a thick gray beard and a mop of Mark Twain–style white hair. He is chewing on the stem of a pipe, one that rarely leaves his mouth, and he is behind an old wooden desk covered with stacks of assorted files and papers. To one side is a battered Royal typewriter, circa 1950, still being used.

"Mr. Casey," he says in a high-pitched, energetic voice as he thrusts forward his right hand. "Clarence Rook."

I shake his hand and say, "Nice to meet you, sir. Thanks for seeing me like this."

"No problem. Have a seat."

I sit in the only chair that is not filled with assorted debris.

"Where you from?" he asks with a smile that reveals a mouthful of tobacco-stained teeth.

"Santa Fe," I say.

"Oh, beautiful country out there. Ms. Rook and I drove out west a few years ago, stopped in Santa Fe to see the O'Keeffe museum. Spectacular country, wouldn't mind living there myself."

"Yes sir, we enjoy it, but you have a pretty nice town here."

"Indeed we do. I was born just up the road in Mountain Home; don't guess I'll ever leave."

"How long have you owned the paper?" I ask in an effort to kill some time with preliminary chitchat. He seems perfectly willing to do the same.

"Bought it twenty years ago from Mrs. Meeks, who owned it forever. She hired me when I was a kid. Never thought I would spend my life publishing a paper, but I've loved every minute of it. So you write too?"

"No sir, I'm not a writer, not a reporter."

The smile vanishes as his eyes narrow and he tries to digest this.

I continue, "And my name is not Paul Casey. It's Paul Tracey."

From a drawer he picks up a pouch of tobacco, slowly fills the bowl of his pipe, tamps it firm, then strikes a match. He never takes his eyes off me, and after he blows a small cloud of smoke, he asks, "Have you ever been told you favor Warren Tracey?"

"I've heard that before, yes."

"Any relation?"

"He's my father."

As expected, this is not well received. For thirty years, I have often hesitated when giving my last name. Usually, it does not get a reaction, but there have been enough uncomfortable moments to render me gun-shy.

He puffs hard for a while, glaring at me, and finally says, "You could get shot around here."

"I didn't come here to get shot, Mr. Rook."

"Why are you here, son?"

"My father is dying of pancreatic cancer. He'll be gone in a few months."

Another puff, another cloud. "I'm sorry," he says, but only to be polite.

"I doubt if this news will cause too much anguish here in Calico Rock," I say.

He nodded and said, "You're right about that. Most folks in these parts would enjoy watching Warren Tracey burn at the stake. And slowly."

"I realize that."

"Does anyone else know you're here?"

"No sir. Only you."

He takes a deep breath and stares at a table lamp, trying to collect his thoughts. A clock on his wall gives him the time as 5:10. I wait, somewhat nervously. He'll either order me out of his office or decide to chat a bit longer. I'm betting on the latter because he is, after all, a reporter and naturally curious.

"Where is your father these days?" he asks.

"Florida. He left the family when I was twelve, and we've had little contact over the years. We're not close, never have been."

"Did he send you here?"

"No sir. He doesn't know."

"May I ask, then, what, exactly, are you doing here?"

"I want to talk to Joe Castle, and I'm hoping that you know the family pretty well."

"Indeed I do, and I know them well enough to tell you that Joe doesn't talk to strangers, and he sure as hell won't talk to the son of Warren Tracey."

62   JOHN GRISHAM

6

Sunday, July 15, 1973. Wrigley Field was once again packed with forty-one thousand fanatics. Another crowd, estimated at ten thousand, mingled outside the stadium looking for tickets, drinking beer, listening to the radio, and in general getting as close as possible to baseball history. Adding to the excitement was the fact that Juan Marichal was starting for the Giants, and his road games generally increased the gate. Though his better years were behind him, Marichal could still beat any team on any day. With his high-kicking windup, superb control, intimidating tactics, and dogged competitiveness, Marichal was colorful and always dangerous. In the previous thirteen years, he had pitched many games at Wrigley, and he had won far more than he had lost.

He wasted no time in causing trouble. When Joe dug in in the bottom of the first, Marichal's first pitch was aimed directly at his shoulder. Joe hit the ground and barely missed being maimed, and Wrigley almost exploded. From the Cubs dugout, there were shouts, threats, lots of cursing at the mound, where Marichal rubbed the baseball, smiled, and considered the next pitch. As a rookie in his fourth game, Joe knew it was not the moment to charge the mound. He had to earn that right, and it would happen soon enough. Keep your cool, his brother Red had advised him. They'll start throwing at you before long.

The next pitch was a fastball, and Joe, swinging from the left side, ripped it down the right field foul line, a screaming bullet that froze the defense and stunned the crowd. The ball was clearly foul, but it kept rising and rising until it

landed high in the upper deck. The pitch
had been outside by six inches and was
traveling at something close to ninety-
five miles an hour, and Joe had easily
yanked it foul. Marichal was impressed.
Willie McCovey took a step back at first,
and Joe noticed this. The third pitch was
a fastball inside. Joe broke with the delivery, his bat trailing. Marichal was at
the end of his theatrical delivery and in
no position to field a bunt. McCovey got
a bad jump. Tito Fuentes raced to cover
first, but to no avail. The ball rolled
through the baseline chalk for forty feet,
then bounced slightly to the left. When
McCovey picked it up, Joe Castle was
sprinting past first base, now fourteen
for fourteen.

McCovey said nothing to the kid.
When the crowd settled down, Marichal
stepped onto the rubber and looked at
Dave Rader behind the plate. He went
into his stretch, kicked high, as always,
and Joe was halfway to second by the
time Marichal released the ball. Rader's
throw to Fuentes was perfect, but much
too late. After a leisurely slide into second, Joe bounced to his feet, looked at

Marichal, shrugged, smiled, and spread his arms as if to say, "You throw at me, I'll make you pay."

Two pitches later, he stole third, then scored on a passed ball.

In the bottom of the fourth, he blooped a single to shallow center for his fifteenth consecutive hit. Marichal then caught him leaning and picked him off first.

As Joe had predicted, they eventually got him out. In his sixteenth at bat, in the bottom of the seventh inning, Joe crushed a ball to deep center, and for a second it looked as if it were gone. But the center fielder, Garry Maddox, drifted back and back until he was on the warning track, then back some more until he was almost touching the ivy. Three hundred ninety-nine feet from home plate, Maddox caught the ball, and the streak was over.

Joe was at second base, jogging, watching Maddox, and when the out was final, he turned and headed to the dugout. The crowd rose again in thunderous applause, and Joe took his time leaving the field.

After the game, the Cubs announced

that his jersey would be changed. Number 42 was set aside, and for the remainder of his brief career Joe Castle wore Number 15.

———

The following Thursday, the Mets began a four-game home series against the Cardinals that was a run-up to the All-Star Game. Of course I knew the pitching rotation. My father was scheduled to get the ball Thursday night, and I wanted to be at Shea Stadium.

Thursday afternoon, before he left for the game, we managed to talk a little baseball. As usual, he was preoccupied and going through his pregame jitters. He was aloof on most days, but when he was about to pitch, he was so distant I wondered if he actually heard my voice. He was thirty-four years old and trying desperately to make something of his declining career. Looking back, I'm sure he was frightened at the prospect of aging out of baseball. The years were slipping by, and the great Warren Tracey was proving to be not so great after all. In the Mets rotation, he was the fourth

man behind Jon Matlack, Jerry Koosman, and the incredible Tom Seaver. As
the teams headed into the All-Star break,
his record was four wins and six losses,
and his earned run average was a
bloated 5.60. The New York sportswriters were demanding a new fourth man.
The Mets were two games under .500
and apparently going nowhere.

"Congratulations on making the All-
Star team," he said. We were on the pa-
tio, in the shade, drinking milk shakes.
He had a banana shake, one he made
himself, precisely six hours before he
took the mound, one of his little quirks.
All baseball players, especially pitchers,
have them, he once told me, so I started
looking for a quirk.

"Thanks. We've been practicing every
day this week. First game's Saturday
against Rye at two o'clock."

"Sorry I can't make it." The Mets
played at the same time Saturday, so
both of us would be happy. He wouldn't
be at my game, and I wouldn't be at his.
"You gonna pitch Saturday?" he asked.

"I doubt it. Right now I'm number two
behind Don Clements. He's twelve."

He couldn't have cared less. He sipped his milk shake and gazed across the lawn, lost in his own world. I really couldn't blame him. On the days I pitched, I thought of nothing else. I could not imagine how nerve-racking it must be to walk to the mound at Shea Stadium in front of fifty thousand fans and perform.

"What about this Joe Castle guy?" I asked.

He snorted his disapproval. "Not a bad start, but these guys flame out. Once or twice around the league, and we figure them out. Every rookie's got a hole in his swing. Sooner or later, we find it."

He seldom said nice things about other players, even his own teammates. At the age of eleven, I thought this was odd, but it would take a few years to understand that he was so insecure about his own game he could rarely admire that of another player.

"Wait until he starts seeing the hard slider," he said, his words trailing off as his mind drifted away.

I wasn't going to argue or cause trou-

ble. I was just thrilled to be talking baseball with my father. "Not a bad start"?
After seven games, Joe had twenty-four
hits in thirty-one at bats, with nine home
runs and nine stolen bases.

"Say, Dad, I would like to see you
pitch tonight. I'll take the train in and
stay out of the way. Tom can come with
me."

He frowned and took another sip.

It would be safe to assume that the
son of a player would have all sorts of
perks, including pregame passes on the
field, locker room clearances, and, of
course, access to tickets. It did not work
that way with Warren Tracey. He did not
want me hanging around and often
complained about other players who let
their kids crawl through the dugout before game time. He considered this to
be highly unprofessional. To him, the
turf was sacred ground, and only those
in uniform should be allowed to step on
it. He flatly refused to speak with any
reporter on the field before a game because, in his opinion, the press should
be confined to the press box.

"I'll see what I can do," he finally said,

as if this were some great favor. My mom would not allow me to ride the train alone, so I had invited Tom Sabbatini.

"I guess your mother's not going to the game," he said.

Talk about a volatile subject. My mother went to a few games each season—as few as possible. We sat with the other Mets families, and I knew some of the players' kids, though we were not friends, because no one else lived in White Plains. My mother refused to socialize with the other wives, and it was many years before she explained why. My father chased women—on the road, at home, in spring training, whenever, wherever, it didn't matter to Warren. My mother knew this, though I'm not sure how she knew. As with every professional baseball team, there were players who fooled around and others who did not. I don't know the percentages, and I doubt if a reliable study has ever been undertaken. Who really wants to know? As my mother explained to me years later, all the wives knew the reputations of the philanderers, and it was safe to

assume that every Mets wife knew Warren Tracey could not keep his pants on.
She felt humiliated sitting in the section
for the players' families with Jill and me
and trying to pretend we were just another happy family.

By July 1973, my parents had endured
twelve years of a bad marriage. Both
were making their own secret exit plans.

That night Tom and I took the train to
Grand Central, then the subway to Shea
Stadium. Our seats were perfect—ten
rows from the field near the Mets dugout. My father pitched well, going six
strong innings and giving up only three
hits, but the Mets blew a two-run lead
in the ninth. On the way home, the subway was filled with rowdy Mets fans,
some of them drunk. Occasionally, on
these trips, or around the Little League
field, or even at school, I would hear
someone complaining about Warren
Tracey. New York sports fans are rabid
and well-informed, and they do not suf-
fer from a lack of opinions. (I was at
Shea once when they booed Tom

Seaver.) Whenever I heard a derogatory comment about my father, I would always flinch and resist the temptation to return the insult. Often, though, the complaints were legitimate.

I made it home, checked in with Mom, then hurried to bed. I did not want to be awake when he got home, if, in fact, he made it back. His worst drunks were on the nights after he pitched. He wouldn't play again for three days, so why not blow it out and raise some hell?

7

The following Saturday, the White Plains East All-Stars lost to Rye in the first round of the regional tournament, and the Mets lost to the Cardinals. I didn't play, and neither did my father. Of course, as a starting pitcher he would never play on his day off, but I should have played an inning or two. During the regular season, when I was not pitching, I roamed the outfield. I hit .412 in eighteen games, sixth highest in the league, and late in the game against Rye we needed a hitter at the plate. Our coach, though, felt otherwise.

Looking at the brackets near the con-
cession stand, I suddenly felt lousy. I
would be the starting pitcher in our next
game Monday afternoon against Eastchester, and my father would be in the
vicinity. He did not make the National
League All-Star team, did not even come
close, though in his opinion he should
have been considered. The All-Star
break ran for three days, with the game
to be played in Kansas City on Tuesday
night.

With a schedule that runs from the
first of April to the end of September,
eighty-one games at home and eighty-
one on the road, big leaguers cherish
the All-Star break. Those not chosen to
play often dash home or enjoy brief va-
cations. The year before, after being
overlooked yet again, my father and a
teammate spent the break trout fishing
in Montana, then met the team in San
Francisco when the schedule resumed.
Listening carefully, I had unfortunately
heard no such talk of a fishing trip this
year.

When my father watched me play, he never sat in the stands with my mother or the other spectators. He didn't want to be bothered. Once, a kid asked for his autograph, and he griped about it for a week. He played for the Mets; therefore, he was famous and did not wish to mingle with ordinary parents. To get away, he would find a spot on the fence not far from our dugout, and from there, alone, he would growl and yell advice. He despised all of my coaches because they, of course, knew so little about the game. Invariably, they tried to engage him because of who he was, and his rude behavior was embarrassing. On several occasions, I was compelled to apologize to a coach.

The tournament was played in Scarsdale, and as we drove to the ballpark, no one said a word in the car. Jill and I were in the rear seat, and she was pouting because she hated baseball. My father was sore because a writer in the *Times* that morning had said the Mets could not win the pennant with Warren Tracey in the rotation. I was a nervous wreck, and my stomach was aching. My mother flipped through a magazine as if all were well.

When I took the mound, I could barely grip the ball. My first pitch was a weak fastball that the batter lined hard, but directly at our shortstop. I took a breath and felt better. My second pitch was a fastball that the batter popped foul to our first baseman. Two pitches—two outs. This might be easier than I thought. The third batter was trouble and everyone knew him. His name was Luke Gozlo, a big kid with a big mouth and a big bat to back up his words. He would later be drafted by the Red Sox and fade away in the minors.

My coach said repeatedly, "Don't put the ball in the center of the plate. A walk is better than a home run." I was trying my best to walk him when my third pitch trailed inside. Luke lifted his front foot, attacked the ball, and as soon as he hit it, I felt sick. Our left fielder never moved. The jackass stood with his hands on his hips and watched the ball as if he were watching a jet fighter buzz the field. It landed in the parking lot. Luke whooped and hollered as he rounded first and second, his fist pumping in the air. What a jerk. He stomped on home plate and yanked off his helmet so everyone could see his grinning face.

I threw three fastballs as hard as I possibly could and struck out the cleanup hitter. As I walked off the field (never run, my father had insisted; the pitcher never runs off the field), my father was waving me over. My coach, though, suspected trouble and met me at the foul line. He put his arm around my shoulder, told me to shake it off, and escorted me into the dugout, where I was safe from my father's advice.

Luke Gozlo came to the plate in the top of the fourth with the bases empty and no outs. My father yelled "Paul" to get my attention, but I pretended not to hear him. My first pitch was a fastball that Luke hacked at and missed, and as our fans were cheering, I heard my father say, "Knock him down, Paul." I looked at my coach. He heard it too, and he was shaking his head. No.

I had hit a few batters, but never intentionally. The year before I had bounced a fastball off the helmet of Kirk Barnes. The sound was sickening. He cried for an hour, and both of us almost quit the game. And I wanted no part of Luke Gozlo. He was a tough kid, the type who would wait in the parking lot after the game and beat the hell out of me.

I walked him on the next four pitches, none of them remotely near his head or near the strike zone. With a 2 and 2 count on the cleanup batter, I hung a curveball, a huge mistake. He crushed it, and when it cleared the fence, Luke started whooping it up and showing his ass again as he rounded the bases. At that moment, I wished I had beaned him.

I struck out the next two, then walked two, then got lucky with a long fly ball to deep right field. As I walked to the dugout, I glanced at my father. He was shaking his head, frowning, mumbling, with both arms folded angrily across his chest. I thought about hitchhiking home. Maybe I could catch a ride with a coach or a teammate. Maybe I could just move in with the Sabbatinis and have a normal life.

With the team trailing 5–2 and facing elimination, our coach decided to change pitchers. I wanted to keep playing, but I was also relieved to be out of the game and tucked away in the dugout.

Eastchester won 11–2, and our season was over.

My career was over too. I would never again put on a baseball uniform.

My father waited perhaps two minutes into the drive home before he reached the point where he could no longer stay quiet. "That was a pathetic game," he began.

My mother was ready to explode, and she snapped, "Don't start it, Warren. Don't even think about it. Just shut up and drive."

I couldn't see his face, but I knew it was bloodred. I knew his first reaction would be to stop the car, slap her across the face, then attack me in the rear seat. Passing motorists would be treated to the sight of another Tracey family brawl, postgame, on the shoulder of the road.

Truthfully, though, he only hit my mother when he was drunk. That was no excuse, but as the seconds ticked by slowly, I was comforted by that fact.

A pathetic game? At that point in his career he had won sixty-one games and lost eighty. What about that pathetic record? What about the pathetic game against the Dodgers back in May when he gave up six runs in the first inning and left with the bases loaded and only one out? What about the pathetic game three weeks ago in Pittsburgh when he took a five-run lead into the seventh inning and blew it before the Mets could warm up a reliever? Don't get me started. I knew his stats better than he did, but if I opened my smart mouth, I knew he would punch me.

I managed to hold my tongue. So did he, and we survived the drive home. As he turned off the ignition, he said, "Let's go to the backyard, Paul, I need to show you something."

I looked at my mother for help, but she was hurrying to get out.

The backyard session turned ugly real fast, then violent. When it was over, I vowed to never play again as long as he was alive.

8

Joe arrived home in the early hours of Monday morning. The lights were on; his parents were waiting. As he parked at the curb, he noticed the large poster staked near the mailbox. It was a replica of the back of a Cubs game jersey with a bold blue Number 15 in the center of it. He looked around—every yard on Church Street had the same poster. Later, he would realize that every front lawn in Calico Rock displayed one too, as well as the windows of every store, office, bank, and café.

His mother's family was from south

Louisiana, and Joe had been raised on Cajun food. His favorite was red beans and rice with andouille sausage, and at three o'clock that morning he devoured a plateful. Then he slept until noon.

Charlie Castle was eight years older than Joe. He was married with two small children and lived in a new home on the edge of town. The family and many friends gathered there late Tuesday afternoon for hot dogs and ice cream. The real purpose, though, was to see Joe, to touch him, to make sure he was real, and to somehow and in some dignified way convey the immense pride they felt. He made it easy. At home, far away from Chicago, far away from anywhere really, the past twelve days seemed surreal, and at times he seemed as dazed as his admirers. He signed autographs, posed for photos, even kissed a few babies. The All-Star Game was on in the den, but everyone was outside.

They had Joe to themselves, but only for a moment. The world was clawing for him. Greatness was waiting, and Joe would soon return to center stage.

I watched the All-Star Game at home with my mother. The Sabbatinis invited me over, but I had a black eye and refused to leave the house. My parents were at war, and eventually my father had fled to the city, where he would no doubt go to a bar and start more trouble. Before he left, he apologized for hitting me, but the apology meant absolutely nothing. I hated the man. I think my mother did too. Jill had long since given up on him.

The game was in Kansas City, and it turned into a celebration of Willie Mays, who was the greatest All-Star performer ever. In a remarkable twenty-four games, he had twenty-three hits, including three home runs, three triples, two doubles, and a highlight reel full of great defensive plays. Now he was forty-two years old, sitting on the bench for the Mets, and planning to retire at the end of the season.

I was the only kid I knew who had actually met Willie Mays. Early in the season, the Mets had their annual family day at Shea Stadium. Most of the players' wives and kids were there to meet each other and pose for photographs. There was ice cream, autographs, tours of the stadium and locker room, and lots of souvenirs. My father had reluctantly allowed me to take part in this wonderful event. I had my picture taken with Willie Mays, Tom Seaver, Rusty Staub, and most of the Mets. My mother had these enlarged to eight by ten, and they were neatly filed away in my scrapbooks. I had thick ones for Tom Seaver and Willie Mays, the only two Mets to make the All-Star team.

As I watched the game, I wondered what they really thought of Warren Tracey. Sure, they were teammates, but I doubted if they cared much for my father. As much as I tried to loosen him up, he rarely talked about the other Mets. He ran around with a couple of relievers from the bull pen, and he would occasionally tell a funny story about something that happened around the clubhouse or on the road—stories that were suitable for our ears. His manager, Yogi Berra, was good for an occasional laugh. But the big Mets—Tom Seaver, Willie Mays, Jerry Koosman, Rusty Staub—were off-limits. Looking back, I think he resented their success.

For the American League, the fans had selected such greats as Brooks Robinson, Reggie Jackson, and Rod Carew. Catfish Hunter started on the mound. In the National League, the Reds had three starters—Pete Rose, Joe Morgan, and Johnny Bench. The Cubs had two—Ron Santo and Billy Williams. Hank Aaron was at first base. A record fifty-four players made it into the game, and I had the Topps baseball card for every one. I knew their ages, birthplaces, heights, weights, and all their stats. I did not deliberately memorize all this data. I simply absorbed it. The game was my world; the players, my idols.

The game, though, had just delivered a nasty blow, and I was a wounded boy. The right side of my face was swollen, and the eye was closed. I was so happy my father was not playing in the All-Star Game, because I would not have been able to endure it. He never came close, though with his twisted ego he felt slighted. It was such a relief to have him out of the house.

My mother sat nearby, reading a paperback, paying no attention to the game, but staying close to me. After he stormed out and things calmed down, she told me that he would never hit me again. I took this to mean she was about to leave him, or he would leave us, or there would be some manner of a breakup. I whispered this to Jill, and we were delighted at first. Then we began to wonder where we would live. What would happen to him? How could Mom survive without his income? As the scenarios unfolded, we had more and more questions, troubling ones. I suppose every kid wants his parents to stay together, but as the day wore on, I found myself torn between the uncertainties of a divorce and the pleasant thoughts of life without my father. I leaned toward the latter.

When Ron Santo walked to the plate in the second inning, Curt Gowdy and Tony Kubek couldn't wait to launch into the Joe Castle story. They had been at Wrigley just ten days earlier for that historic event and recapped it as Santo worked the count off Catfish Hunter. After eleven games, Joe had forty at bats, twenty-nine hits, twelve home runs, and fourteen stolen bases. He had hit safely in every game, and, more important, the Cubs had won nine of the eleven and were in first place in the National League East. Wrigley Field had sold out not only for each of the six games Joe had played there but for every game until after Labor Day.

Kubek offered the same speculation that was making the rounds. The wise men of baseball, including my father, were predicting that the pitchers would soon catch on to Joe and find his weaknesses. His current batting average of .725 was ridiculous and certain to plummet as he made his way around the league.

Gowdy was not so sure. "I didn't notice any holes in his swing," he said.

"Nor did I," Kubek quickly agreed.

"He's struck out only twice."

"Great balance; he stays back, incredible bat speed."

Poor Ron Santo was overshadowed

by his rookie teammate who, at that moment, was eating his aunt Rachel's homemade strawberry ice cream in Calico Rock, Arkansas, and oblivious to the game.

When play resumed on July 26, the Cubs opened a four-game series in Cincinnati against the Big Red Machine, the most dominant team of the 1970s. With a lineup that included Pete Rose, Johnny Bench, Joe Morgan, and Tony Perez, the Reds narrowly lost the 1972 World Series in seven games to the A's, then won it all in 1975 and 1976.

They were leading the Dodgers by two games in the National League West. As usual, a large crowd was on hand, and most were curious to see if the bat of Joe Castle had cooled off during the All-Star break.

It had not. Joe hit a solo home run in his first at bat and barely missed another one in the fourth inning. He was three for four in game one; two for five in game two; two for four in game three; and one for three in game four. The teams split the series, and the Reds would go on to win ninety-nine games and take the National League West. For the series, Joe went eight for sixteen, and his average dropped to .661.

Another obscure record was suddenly in sight. In 1941, a Red rookie by the name of Chuck Aleno made a dazzling debut by hitting safely in his first seventeen games, a modern-day record that stood until 1973. Aleno cooled off considerably and left baseball three years later after playing in only 118 games and hitting .209. The experts, of course, were still predicting such a collapse for Joe Castle.

Joe's sixteenth game was in Pittsburgh, and he got things started in the top of the first with a stand-up triple. The crowd, and the Cubs were drawing well on the road, applauded politely. Pirates fans had been spoiled with the likes of Roberto Clemente, Willie Stargell, and Al Oliver, and they knew their baseball. They were watching history, and though they wanted a win, they were also pulling for this new kid. The second game went fourteen innings; Joe got five hits in seven at bats. He tied Aleno's record with a home run in his seventeenth game, then broke it with two doubles in his eighteenth.

When the Cubs left Pittsburgh for a three-game series in Montreal, Joe had played in nineteen games, had hit safely in each, and was sporting a gaudy batting average of .601, with fourteen home runs and seventeen stolen bases. Records were still falling; baseball had never seen such a furious start by a rookie.

The Cubs were the hottest team in baseball and led the Pirates in the East by six games.

———

The August 6 issue of *Sports Illustrated* had on its cover the smiling face of Joe Castle. The photo was shot from the waist up. A baseball bat ran the length of his broad shoulders, and he held both ends tightly with his hands. His biceps were sufficiently flexed—it was the look of raw power. The bold caption above his head read: "Calico

Joe." And below his chest—"The Phenom."

The writer spent time in Calico Rock.
He interviewed Joe's family, friends, and
former coaches and teammates. The
article was thorough, fair, and balanced
and provided the first in-depth look at
Joe's background. A valuable source
was Clarence Rook, sports editor of the
Calico Rock Record and unofficial baseball historian for Izard County, Arkansas.

9

Mr. Clarence Rook asks me to leave the newspaper's offices on Main Street, and I do so. I have two scoops of vanilla at an ice cream shop two doors down and listen to some casual town gossip as I watch the languid foot traffic on the sidewalk. After killing an hour, I drive three blocks west and higher up the bluff to a house at 130 South Street where Mr. Rook has lived for the past forty-one years. He is waiting, standing on the front porch, already in his drinking clothes.

The house is a rambling old Victorian,

with wide, sweeping covered porches, high arching windows, painted gables, all different colors, the most dominant being a soft pastel maize. The small lawn and flower beds are as neat and colorful as the house.

"A beautiful place," I say as I walk through the swinging gate of a white picket fence.

"It's a hand-me-down. My wife's family. Welcome."

He is wearing a white linen shirt with a tail that falls almost to his knees, a pair of bulky white britches that bunch around his bare ankles, and a pair of well-worn and scuffed espadrilles. He is holding a tall, slender beverage glass with a straw in his right hand, and with his left he waves at the side porch and says, "Follow me. Fay's back there somewhere." I follow him over the creaking boards and under the whirling ceiling fans. The porch is crowded with white wicker furniture—rockers, stools, drink tables, a long swing covered with pillows.

Fay is Ms. Rook, a spry little woman with white hair and a pair of large, round, orange-rimmed glasses. She welcomes me profusely, grabbing my hand with both of hers, as if she has not had a guest in years. "From Santa Fe?" she says. "I love Santa Fe, the home of the most fascinating woman I wish I could have met."

"And that would be?"

"Why Georgia O'Keeffe, of course."

"Fay is an artist," Mr. Rook adds, though this is becoming obvious. We are on the back porch by now, high above the White River in the distance, and I have unknowingly entered the studio of a serious painter. Stacks of easels, racks of perfectly organized paint bottles, boxes of brushes of all sizes and shapes. A few samples of her work reveal an impressionist fascination with flowers and landscapes.

"Would you like something to drink?" Mr. Rook asks as he steps to a small bar.

"Sure."

"The house drink is lemon gin," he says as he pours a yellow mix from a pitcher into a glass filled with ice. I have never heard of lemon gin, but it is apparent I will not be given a choice of cocktails.

"That stuff is dreadful," Ms. Rook says, rolling her eyes as if the old boy might have a problem. He thrusts the glass at me and says, "It's not real lemon gin, which I'm told is real gin flavored with lemon, which sounds awful, but this is more of a lemonade with a bit of Gordon's thrown in to spice it up. Cheers."

We tap glasses, and I take a sip. Not bad. We shuffle to the side porch and find seats amid the wicker. Ms. Rook is a study in bright colors. Her white hair has a streak of purple above the left ear. Her toenails are painted pink. Her cotton drip-dry dress is a collage of reds and blues. "You must stay for dinner," she says. "We eat from the garden, everything is fresh. No meats. Is that okay?"

There was no way to offer a polite no, and besides, I have already realized that a good restaurant might be hard to find in Calico Rock. Nor have I seen a motel.

"If you insist," I say, and this seems to thrill her beyond words.

"I'll go pick the squash," she says, bouncing to her feet and hurrying away.

We sip our drinks and talk about the heat and humidity but soon find our way back to more important matters. He begins, "You have to understand, Paul, that the Castles are very protective of Joe. If you met him, let's say randomly, out there on the street, for example, though that would never happen because Joe is seldom seen around town, but, anyway, if you bumped into him and tried to say hello, he would simply walk away. I can't imagine Joe chatting with a stranger. It just doesn't happen. Over the years, we've had the occasional journalist show up looking for a story. There were a couple of pieces written a long time ago, and they said things that weren't nice."

"Such as?"

"Joe is brain damaged. Joe is disabled. Joe is bitter. And so on. The family is very distrustful of anyone who shows up and wants to talk about Joe. That's why they would never allow him to speak to you."

"Could I talk to his brothers?"

"Who am I? You're on your own, but I wouldn't recommend it. Red and Charlie are nice enough, but they can be tough guys. And when it comes to their little brother, they can turn nasty real quick. They carry guns, like a lot of people around here. Hunting rifles and such."

The lemon gin is settling in, and I want to change the subject to anything but guns. I take a long sip, as does Mr. Rook, and for a moment the only sounds are the whirling blades of the ceiling fans. Finally, I ask, "Did you see him play at Wrigley?"

A wide, nostalgic smile breaks across his face, and he begins to nod. "Twice. Fay and I drove to Chicago early in August of that summer. The *Sports Illustrated* piece had just been published, and the world couldn't get enough of Joe Castle."

"How did you get tickets?"

"Scalpers. There were a lot of folks around here who wanted desperately to get to Chicago for a game, but word was out that you couldn't get tickets. Joe got a handful each game, and there was always a fight for those. I remember drinking coffee one morning downtown and Mr. Herbert Mangrum walked in. He had some money, and he had just flown to Pittsburgh to watch the Cubs. Said he had to pay a scalper $300 for two tickets, in Pittsburgh. Herb was a big talker, and he went on and on about seeing Joe in Pittsburgh."

"So you drove to Chicago with no tickets?"

"That's right, but I had a contact. We got lucky and saw two games. Spoke to Joe after the first one. The kid was on top of the world. We were so proud."

"Which games?"

"August 9 and 10, against the Braves."

"You missed the fun. He got ejected the next day."

Mr. Rook licks his lips, cocks his head, and gives me a strange look. "You know your stuff, don't you?"

"Yes sir, I do."

"Could you please drop the 'sirs' and the 'misters'? I'm Clarence, and my wife is Fay."

"Okay, Clarence. What do you want

to know about the short, happy, and tragic career of Joe Castle?"

"How many games did he play?" Clarence asks, knowing the answer.

"Thirty-eight, and I have the box score for every one. He would've played forty-three but for the ejection on August 11, the day after you saw him play."

Clarence smiles, nods, takes a long sip, and says, "You're wrong, Paul. He would've played three thousand games if he hadn't been beaned." He sets his drink on the table, stands, and says, "I'll be right back."

He returns with a cardboard box, which he sets on the floor next to his sofa. From it he removes four thick three-ring binders, all matched and perfectly organized. He places them on the wicker table and says, "This is the book I never wrote—the story of Joe Castle. Many years ago, I started the first chapter, then put it aside. This is not the only unfinished project, mind you, in fact there are many, and I suppose the world is a better place because of my tendency to procrastinate."

"How can a newspaper editor procrastinate? Doesn't your life revolve around deadlines?"

"Some deadlines, sure, but because we stare at the calendar all day long, we tend to shove aside our other projects."

"So why didn't you write this book?"

"Truthfully, it was the family. I talked to Red one time, and he didn't like the idea. This town is too small to make enemies, and if the family wasn't willing to cooperate, then the book was not worth writing." He flips through the second binder and finds the tab for August 11, 1973. "Sit over here," he says, patting a spot next to him. I move around to take a look, eager to see his research.

"This is one of my favorite stories," he says, pointing to an article in the *Tribune* about Joe getting ejected for charging the mound. There was a large photo of a brawl. "By early August of that summer, the pitchers were throwing at Joe more and more. It's part of the ritual of being a rookie, especially one who happens to be on a tear. But the Cubs had Ferguson Jenkins and Rick Reuschel, two tough guys who threw hard and were known to protect their hitters.

There were rumors that Jenkins and Reuschel and some of the other Cubs
pitchers had spread the word that if Joe
got hit, the retaliation would be swift. As
things turned out, Joe didn't need any
help. The Braves had a journeyman lefty
named Dutch Patton, a big thick guy,
six five or so, and the first time up Joe
ripped a double, then stole third. We
were still in Chicago but couldn't get
tickets to the game, so we were watching on television. When Joe came up in
the third inning, Patton threw at his head
and almost nailed him. The Cubs dugout went berserk; the fans were ready
to riot. Joe yelled something at Patton,
and he yelled something back. The
home plate umpire got involved. A very
tense situation. Joe got back in the box,
dug in, and Patton went into his windup.
Just as he released the ball, Joe dropped
his bat and sprinted toward the mound.
He was so quick and fast he caught everybody—including Patton and the
catcher, Johnny Oates—completely off
guard. I've seen the film clip a hundred
times, and what happened was pretty
frightening. Patton managed to swing

his glove at Joe, who ducked and shot a right cross into Patton's mouth. A left hook to the nose knocked him down and, like a jackhammer, Joe pummeled him with five more shots to the face, each one drawing blood. Patton left the field on a stretcher, didn't wake up for six hours, and didn't pitch for a month. Johnny Oates finally managed to pull Joe off, and by then there were forty players on the field slugging it out. The brawl lasted for ten minutes, and there were something like seven or eight ejections. Joe was suspended for five games, and the Cubs lost all five."

As he talks, I listen intently and flip through his binder. I have a copy of the *Tribune* story, along with the photo, but my little scrapbook on Joe Castle is nothing compared with the spread before me. I know the story of Joe's retaliation against Dutch Patton, and Clarence has not missed a detail.

"What was so funny, at least to me, was that I had seen Joe pull the same trick before," Clarence is saying.

"When?" I ask as he pauses and waits for me to prompt him.

"When he was seventeen, in a high school game against Heber Springs. Scouts all over the place, all here to see Joe. First time up, he hit a ball over the lights in right field. The second time up, the pitcher threw at his head. He kept his cool, waited. When you charge the mound, your biggest threat is being tackled from behind by the catcher. All three of the Castle boys understood this rather basic part of the game. Joe waited until the pitch was thrown, then sprinted to the mound. It was pretty ugly. These were kids, and the benches did not empty as fast as they do in the big leagues . . ." Clarence's words trail off as though he doesn't want to finish the story.

"Did he hurt the pitcher?"

"Let's just say the kid didn't pitch for a few days, maybe weeks, maybe never, I don't know, but I'm sure he lost his enthusiasm for throwing beanballs. Joe was not a bully, just the opposite; he was a really nice kid. But he didn't like guys throwing at him."

"Who broke up the fight?"

"The umpires. No player on the other team wanted to get near it."

I flip back and forth and come across the cover of *Sports Illustrated*. "I'll bet this caused some excitement around here."

"Oh yes, not that there was a lack of excitement that summer. Everybody in town wanted to talk to the reporter. Let me refresh your drink there, Paul." He takes both glasses to the back porch. I follow and peek into the kitchen, where Fay is slicing eggplant. When the drinks are ready, Clarence repacks his pipe and lights it. With fresh lemon gins in hand, we walk down the rear steps and gaze at the White River.

"Where did the nickname come from?" I ask.

Clarence chuckles and takes a sip. "*Sports Illustrated*, I guess. That's the first time I ever heard of Calico Joe. But it stuck. The Chicago writers ran with it and never looked back. They had Shoeless Joe a half century earlier, so I guess it was irresistible."

"It's such a perfect nickname."

"It is, or was."

We watch two men in a boat cast their lines and drift with the current.

"What does Joe do around here?" I ask.

"He takes care of his baseball field."

"His field?"

"Yes. Joe Castle Field, over at the high school. He mows the grass every morning. He rakes the dirt, pulls weeds, lays the chalk, sweeps the dugouts, and in general putters around the field five days a week. If it snows, Joe scrapes it off the bleachers. When it's raining, he sits in the dugout, third base side, and watches the puddles form around the infield. When it stops raining, he gently spreads the dirt around so there will be no puddles the next time. About this time of year, after summer ball is over, he'll paint both dugouts and the press box. It's his field."

"Can I see him tomorrow?"

"Again, I'm not his keeper. You can do whatever you want."

"But would he speak to me?"

"I've already explained that, Paul. Joe doesn't speak to strangers."

"Would he speak to my father, if I brought him here?"

Clarence coughed and glared at me as if I had insulted his wife. "Are you crazy?"

"Maybe. He's dying, Clarence, and before he's gone, I would like for the two men to have a word."

"What kind of word?"

"I'm not sure, but ideally I would like my father to apologize."

"Have you discussed this with your father?"

"No, not yet, and before I do, I need to know if Joe will agree to a meeting."

"I doubt seriously if that can happen, Paul. And it would be a huge mistake for Warren Tracey to show up here in Calico Rock. That could start some serious trouble."

10

It took a week for the black eye to fade away, and I spent most of the time in my room, reading and looking in the mirror. My father stopped by twice with clumsy efforts at making peace, but I was not in the mood. When you get backhanded by your father, the pain lasts far longer than the bruises. Mercifully, the Mets left town for a long road trip, and I ventured out of my room and tried to enjoy the last month of my summer break.

On August 8, the Mets shut out the Astros in Houston. My father pitched seven innings, gave up only three hits, walked only two, and won his fifth game of the season. I listened to the game in the den and, as usual, recorded every pitch and play on my official Mets score-card. I knew it was his best game in many years, and as Lindsey Nelson and Ralph Kiner said nice things about my father, I couldn't help but feel a tiny bit of pride, although grudgingly. I was get-ting in bed when he called home and wanted to chat about the game. We stayed on the phone for half an hour as he recounted the highlights and patiently answered my questions, and when we eventually said good night, I was so ex-cited I had trouble sleeping. Four days later, he pitched a complete-game four-hitter against the Padres for his second win in a row, a rare feat for Warren Tracey. Because he was on the West Coast, he did not call me after the game, but late the next morning he checked in from his hotel room, and we talked for almost an hour.

My mother was happy because I was happy, but she was also suspicious about his sudden interest in me. My bruises were gone, and the emotional scars were fading, or so I thought.

In the New York papers, the battle was still raging over Warren Tracey and whether he should get benched or sent down. His two consecutive wins cooled his critics but did little to arouse any support. The Mets were coming to life, though it looked as if no team could catch the Cubs. Joe Castle was still red-hot and front-page news in Chicago and wherever he happened to be playing.

I made the calculations a dozen times, and assuming no sudden changes in the pitching rotations, the lineups, injuries, or disruptions due to weather, the Cubs would arrive at Shea Stadium on Friday, August 24. Joe Castle would make his New York debut, and my father would be on the mound. The Cubs would be in first place in the East, and the Mets, in all likelihood, would be in second. When I considered this, and I did so at least ten times each day that August, my stomach would tie itself in knots, and I could not swallow water. Warren Tracey versus Joe Castle. My feelings for my father were hopelessly mixed and confused. For the most part, I despised him; yet he was my father, and he was a professional baseball player pitching for the New York Mets! How many eleven-year-old boys could make such a claim? We lived in the same house. We had the same ancestors, name, address. His success or failure had a direct impact on me. I adored his parents, though I rarely saw them. He was my father, damn it! I wanted him to win.

However, the world of baseball was revolving around Joe Castle. He sold out wherever he went, and the seats were often filled during pregame batting practice. He was hounded by reporters so fiercely that he was hiding from them. On the road, fans flocked to the Cubs' hotels hoping for an autograph or a glimpse. Young women were sending all types of proposals, marriage and otherwise. His teammates and coaches were devising schemes to protect his privacy. Insanity ruled off the field, but between the chalk lines Joe Castle continued to play like a kid on a sandlot. He sprinted after foul balls, lunged into the stands, turned lazy singles into doubles, bunted with two strikes, violently broke up double plays, tagged up on every fly ball to the outfield, usually had the dirtiest uniform when the game was over, and through it all ripped baseballs to all corners of the field.

The thought of Joe digging in against my father was overwhelming, but as the long hot days of August moved along, I found myself thinking of nothing else. My buddies were hounding me for tickets. The four games against the Cubs were sold out. New York was waiting.

———

His five-game suspension for punching out Dutch Patton ended on August 17, and with a talent for the dramatic Joe returned to a raucous Wrigley Field for an afternoon game against the Dodgers. He singled in the first, doubled in the fourth, tripled in the seventh, and when he stepped to the plate in the bottom of the ninth, he only needed a home run to complete the cycle. The Cubs needed a home run to win the game. Batting right-handed, he poked a blooper down the right field line, and as it rolled slowly to the wall, the race was on. Ron Santo scored easily from second with the tying run, and when Joe sprinted to third, he ignored the coach's signal to stop. He never slowed down. The short-stop took the relay, looked at third, where Joe would have an easy triple, then hesitated at the sight of him streak-ing home. The throw was perfect, and the catcher, Joe Ferguson, snatched it and blocked the plate. Ferguson was six feet two, 200 pounds. Joe was six feet two, 185 pounds. In a split-sec-ond decision, neither chose to yield an inch. Joe lowered his head, left his feet, and crashed into Ferguson. The colli-sion was thunderous and spun both players in violent circles in the dirt. Joe would've been out by three feet, but the ball was loose and rolling in the grass.

It was an inside-the-park home run, his first, and it was a miracle that both he and Ferguson walked away from the collision, though both did so rather slowly.

After thirty-one games, he had sixty-two hits in 119 at bats, with eighteen

home runs and twenty-five stolen bases.
He had made one error at first and had
struck out only six times. His batting average of .521 was easily the highest in
the majors, though he had not had
enough at bats to qualify for the official
ranking. As expected, his average was
slowly declining.

Ty Cobb, the greatest hitter of all time,
had a career average of .367. Ted Williams—.344. Joe DiMaggio—.325. Joe
Castle was not yet being compared to
the great ones, but no rookie had ever
hit .521 after 119 at bats.

On August 20, the Mets were at home
against the Cardinals, and my father
was starting. After winning two in a row,
he had lost a one-run game to the Dodgers and got roughed up by the Giants
but avoided taking the loss. His record
was six and seven, and he was feeling
good about his game. After his banana
milk shake, he asked me if I would like
to ride with him to Shea Stadium. This,
of course, meant that I would be allowed
to hang around the locker room, dug-

out, and field for hours before the first pitch. I jumped at the chance. He promised to drive me home after the game, which, of course, meant he would not be hitting the bars. The tension around the house had thawed somewhat. My parents were civil to each other, at least in the presence of Jill and me. For two uncertain kids, this only confused matters.

I was in the Mets dugout, watching the Cardinals take batting practice, soaking in the sights and sounds, reveling in the rarest of moments, when Willie Mays walked by and said, "Hey, kid, what brings you here?"

"My dad's pitching," I said, thoroughly awestruck.

"Tracey?"

"Yes sir."

And then Willie Mays sat down beside me on the bench as if time meant nothing. He said, "I can't remember your name."

"Paul Tracey," I said.

"Nice to see you again, Paul."

I tried to say something but froze.

"Your dad's pitching well these days," he said. "Seems like he told me you're a pitcher too."

"Yes sir, but our season's over. I'll be twelve next year."

Lou Brock was in the cage for the Cardinals, spraying baseballs everywhere. We watched him take a dozen swings, then Willie spoke to another player who walked in front of us. When we were alone again, he said, "You know, I never wanted to pitch. You gotta rely on too many other players to succeed. You can be having a great day on the mound, then, just like that, somebody makes an error and you lose the game, you know?"

"Yes sir." I would agree with anything Mr. Mays had to say.

"Or you strike out twenty, give up two hits, and lose the game one to nothing, you know what I'm saying, Paul?"

"Yes sir."

"Plus, I could never throw strikes, which is tough when you're trying to pitch."

"I've had that problem occasionally," I

said, and Willie Mays laughed out loud. He tapped me on the knee and said, "Good luck to you, Paul."

"Thanks, Mr. Mays."

He jumped to his feet and was yelling at one of the Cardinals. I looked at my knee for a long time and vowed to never wash that pair of jeans. A few minutes later, Wayne Garrett and Ed Kranepool sat nearby and began watching batting practice. I inched a bit closer so I could eavesdrop.

"You hear what Castle did today?" Garrett asked as he chomped on bubble gum.

"No," Kranepool replied.

"Four for four with two doubles, off Don Sutton."

"Off Sutton?" Kranepool asked in disbelief.

"Yep. I thought the kid was cooling off."

"Guess not. Should be a wild weekend around here. You got any spare tickets?"

"Are you kidding?"

I sat alone eight rows from the field and close to the Mets dugout. My father gave up a home run to Joe Torre in the first inning, then settled down and pitched well. He ran out of gas in the top of the seventh, with the Mets leading 5–2, and when Yogi Berra pulled him, he received an impressive ovation from the crowd. I was on my feet, clapping and yelling as loud as possible. He tipped his cap to me, and at that moment I realized how much I wanted to adore him.

His record was seven and seven. His next start would be against the Cubs.

11

After two lemon gins, I am sufficiently mellow and want no more. Clarence seems unfazed by the booze, and when he goes for his third, I decline and ask for water. Fay is buzzing about, cooking and setting the table on the back porch. The sun is falling, and its last rays glisten across the White River below us. Clarence and I sit under a maple tree next to the vegetable garden and talk about the Castle boys.

Their grandfather, Vick Castle, signed with the Cleveland Indians in 1906 and five years later made it to the big leagues, but for less than a month. He played in ten games before being sent down. After the season he was traded, then broke an ankle, and his career fizzled. He returned to Izard County and ran a sawmill before dying at the age of forty-four. Bobby, his only son and Joe's father, signed with Pittsburgh in 1938, and in 1941 he led the AAA International League in hitting and RBIs. He was destined to start at third base for the Pirates in 1942, but the war got in the way. He joined the Navy and was shipped to the Pacific, where he lost half a leg to a land mine.

His oldest son, Charlie, signed out of high school with the Washington Senators and bounced around the minors for six years before he called it quits. Red, the middle brother, signed with the Phillies in 1966 but couldn't get out of single A. He quit, joined the Marines, and volunteered for two tours of duty in Vietnam.

Clarence enjoys his narrative and does not need notes. I am amazed at his ability to recall, though I have no way of knowing his level of accuracy. There

is something about his twinkling eyes
and bushy eyebrows that leads me to
believe that this guy is not beyond em-
bellishment. But it doesn't matter; he
loves to talk and tell stories, and the
Castle family is obviously a favorite topic.
I am delighted to be here and happy to
listen.

"Even when Charlie and Red were
playing," he is saying, "everyone was
talking about Joe. When he was ten or
so, a little fellow, he hit four home runs
in a game against Mountain Home. That
was the first time he got his name in the
newspaper. I went to the archives and
pulled it out. In 1973, I got flooded with
folks wanting all sorts of background on
Joe Castle. I spent half the summer digging through back copies. When he was
twelve, he led our All-Stars to a third-
place finish in Little Rock, and I ran this
huge front-page story about the team,
big photo and all. When he was thirteen,
he stopped playing with the kids and
spent all summer with a men's team.
Joe played first, Red at second, three
and four in the lineup, and they must've
played a hundred games. That's when

we realized he might be special. The scouts began showing up when he was fifteen. Charlie was in the minors. Red was in the minors. But everybody was talking about Joe. I was covering a state play-off game in May 1968, down in Searcy, and he hit a baseball that bounced off a school bus in a parking lot, 420 feet from home plate. Can you imagine? A sixteen-year-old kid hitting a 420-foot home run, with wood, not aluminum. The scouts were drooling, shaking their heads in disbelief. Pretty amazing."

"Clarence, dinner is ready," Fay yells from the porch, and we do not waste time. That barbecue pork sandwich for lunch was now at least eight hours in the past. Directly under a ceiling fan, Fay has set a beautiful table, small and round, with fresh-cut flowers in a small vase in the center. There is a large bowl of tomato, cucumber, and onion salad and another of grilled squash and eggplant over brown rice. She waves at the food and says, "Two hours ago, it was still on the vine."

We pass the bowls and begin eating.

I feel compelled to at least make an effort to discuss her art but decide against it. A visit like this will never be repeated, and I want to hear and talk about Joe Castle. After some chatter about my wife, daughters, and job, I manage to get things back on track.

"What was it like in 1970 when the draft was approaching?" I ask.

Clarence chews, swallows, takes a sip of water, and says, "Pretty crazy. We thought he would be the number one pick in the draft, at least that's what the scouts had been saying for two years."

"The town thought he was about to get rich," Fay adds.

"Top money back then was $100,000 for the early picks. In case you haven't noticed, this is a small town. Folks were openly discussing what Joe might do with all his money. Then something weird happened. In late May, Calico Rock was playing in the finals of the state tournament, over at Jonesboro, and Joe had two bad games. He had not had a bad game in ten years, then bam, two in a row. Some of the scouts got spooked, I guess. The Cubs took him in the second round, offered him $50,000, and away he went."

"What happened to the money?" I ask.

"He gave $5,000 to his church," Fay says, "and $5,000 to the high school, right, Clarence?"

"That sounds right. Another $5,000 went to dress up the Little League park where he had played so many games. Seems like he paid off the mortgage on his parents' home, which wasn't that much."

"No shiny new Corvette?" I ask.

"Oh no. He paid $2,000 for Hank Thatcher's Ford pickup. Hank had just died, and his wife was selling some of his stuff. She didn't want the truck, so Joe bought it."

I remind myself, again, of why I do not want to live in a small town. Such personal details would never be discussed, or even known, in a city.

I cannot remember the last time I have eaten vegetables as fresh as Fay's. Sara cooks healthy meals, but I have never tasted squash and eggplant like this.

"Delicious," I say for the second or third time.

"Thank you," Fay replies graciously. I notice that she eats very little. Clarence washes his food down with water, but the lemon gin is still close. Two fishing boats float quietly by on the river and head for the docks below the bridge in the distance. Our conversation drifts to Fay's sister, who is dying of cancer in Missouri and wants them to visit her over the weekend. The cancer talk brings things around to my father. "When was he diagnosed?" Fay asks.

"Last week. It's terminal, just a few months, maybe weeks."

"I'm so sorry," she says.

"Have you seen him?" Clarence asks.

"No, I'm going down tomorrow. As I said, we're not close, not close at all. Never have been. He left the family when his baseball career flamed out and soon remarried. He's not a nice person, Clarence, not the kind of guy you'd want to spend time with."

"I believe that. I read a story about him years ago. After baseball, he tried to make it as a golfer, but that went nowhere. Seems like he was selling real estate in the Orlando area and not doing very well. He was still adamant that he did not throw at Joe, but the writer was skeptical. I guess we're all skeptical."

"You should be," I say.

"Why is that?"

I wipe my mouth with a linen napkin. "Because he threw at Joe. I know he did. He's denied it for thirty years, but I know the truth."

There is a long pause as we pick at our food and listen to the whirling of the old ceiling fan just above us. Finally, Clarence lifts his lemon gin and gulps down an ounce. He licks his lips, smacks them, and says, "You have no idea how excited we were, how much it meant to this town and especially to the family. After producing so many great players, a Castle had finally hit the big time."

"I wish I could say I'm sorry."

"You can't. Besides, it was thirty years ago."

"A long time," Fay observes as she looks down at the river. A long time, maybe, but never to be forgotten.

"I don't suppose you were there," Clarence says.

"Indeed I was. August 24, 1973. Shea Stadium."

12

My father was in a foul mood when he left the house, alone. I dropped a few hints about riding to the stadium with him, but he wasn't listening. The New York papers were relentlessly hyping the game, and one writer, my father's loudest critic, described the matchup as "a contrast between youth and age. Warren Tracey, age thirty-four and over the hill, versus Joe Castle, the brightest young star baseball has seen since the arrival of Mickey Mantle in 1951."

Jill was away at a camp in the Catskills. I cajoled my mother into taking an early train to the city. I wanted to watch batting practice and, more important, get my first live look at Joe Castle. We stepped off the subway at 4:30, two and a half hours before the first pitch, and the atmosphere outside Shea Stadium was electric. I was surprised at the number of Cubs fans, most of them wearing white jerseys with the Number 15 across the back. Some were families who were well behaved, but many were young men in packs roaming around like street gangs, yelling, drinking beer, looking for trouble. They found it. New York fans are far from shy and seldom back down from a challenge. I saw the police break up three fights before we passed through the turnstiles. "Disgusting," my mother said. It would be her last trip to the ballpark.

Shea held fifty-five thousand, and it was already two-thirds full when we settled into our seats. The Cubs were taking batting practice, and there was a swarm around the cage at home plate. Ron Santo, Billy Williams, Jose Cardenal, and Rick Monday were in one group, and as they rotated through, I searched the outfield until I saw him. As he turned to chase a fly ball, I saw the name Castle across the back of his royal blue hitting jersey. He caught the ball near the right field foul line, and a thousand kids screamed for his autograph. He smiled and waved and jogged back to a group of Cubs loitering in right center, probably talking about the women up in the outfield bleachers.

By then, I had read many descriptions of Joe Castle. In high school, some scouts had worried that he was too thin. He weighed 170 pounds when he was eighteen, and this had bothered a few of the experts. However, his father had been quoted as saying, "He's not even shaving yet. Let the boy grow up." And he was right. In the minors, Joe had filled out, thanks to a combination of nature and hours in the weight room. He had broad shoulders and a thirty-three-inch waist. He wore his game pants tight, and one article in the *Tribune* gossiped about the avalanche of provocative mail he was getting from women across the country.

As I watched, he seemed to glide

across the outfield as the bats cracked
and baseballs flew everywhere. I saw
my father in the Mets dugout, sitting
alone, going through his pregame ritual.
It was far too early for him to head to
the bull pen and begin stretching. Odd,
though, that he was in the dugout. Usually, at two hours and counting, he was
in the locker room getting a massage
from a trainer. With ninety minutes to
go, he put on his uniform. At seventy-
five minutes, he left the locker room,
walked through the dugout, and headed
for the bull pen, head down, refusing to
look at the opposing dugout. The more
I thought about it, the stranger it seemed.
Baseball players, and especially pitchers, are fanatics about their rituals. My
father was three and one in his last six
starts and four days earlier had pitched
perhaps his best game in the last five
years. Why would he change things?

My mother bought me a souvenir pro-
gram, then some ice cream, and I chatted with the fans around me. Eventually,
Joe drifted to the Cubs dugout opposite
where we were sitting. He got his bats,
put on his helmet, and began limbering

up. To get away from the stands, he stayed close to the batting cage. When it was his turn, he jumped in, bunted a few, then began spraying the ball to all fields. Bodies moved closer to the cage. Photographers were scrambling into position and clicking away. In his second round, he cranked it up, and the balls went deeper and deeper. He unloaded in his third round, from both sides of the plate, and hit five straight bombs into the bleachers, where hundreds of kids scrambled to get the souvenirs. The Cubs fans were screaming with each shot, and I would have cheered too, but I was in the Mets section; plus, my father was the opposing pitcher, and it did not seem appropriate.

When he walked to the mound in the top of the first, the fans gave him a rowdy welcome. There was not an empty seat in the stadium, and for over an hour the Cubs and Mets fans had been yelling back and forth. When Rick Monday lined to short on the first pitch, the stadium roared again. Two pitches later, Glenn Beckert popped out to right field, and Warren Tracey was cruising.

The announcer said: "Now batting and playing first base, Number 15, Joe Castle."

I took a deep breath and began chewing my fingernails. I wanted to watch, then I wanted to close my eyes and just listen. My mother patted my knee. I envied her apathy. At that crucial moment in my life, in the life of her husband, in the lives of countless Mets and Cubs fans across the country, at that wonderfully supercharged moment in the history of baseball, my mother could not have cared less what happened next.

Not surprisingly, the first pitch was high and tight. Joe, batting left-handed, ducked but did not fall; nor did he glare at my father. It was a simple brushback. Welcome to New York. The second pitch was a called strike that looked low, but Joe did not react. The third pitch was a fastball that he slapped into the stands near us. The fourth pitch was low and inside. The fifth pitch was a changeup that fooled Joe, but he managed to foul it off.

I was holding my breath with each pitch. I was praying for a strikeout, and

I was praying for a home run. Why couldn't I have both? A strikeout now for my father, a home run later for Joe, back and forth? In baseball, you always get another chance, right? I pondered these things between pitches, a complete nervous wreck.

The sixth pitch was a curve that bounced in the dirt. Three balls, two strikes. Billy Williams on deck. Shea Stadium rocking. The Cubs ten games in first place. The Mets ten games back but winning. My father versus my hero.

Joe fouled off the next eight pitches as the at bat turned into a dramatic duel, with neither player yielding an inch. Warren Tracey was not about to walk him. Joe Castle was not about to strike out. The fifteenth pitch was a fastball that looked low, but at the last second Joe whipped his bat around, scooped the ball up, and launched it to right center, where it cleared the wall by thirty feet. For some reason, when I knew the ball was gone, I looked back at the mound and watched my father. He never took his eyes off Joe as he rounded first, and when the ball cleared the fence, Joe gave himself a quick pump of the fist, as if to say, "All right!" It was nothing cocky or out of line, nothing meant to show up the pitcher.

But I knew my father, and I knew it was trouble.

The home run was Joe's twenty-first home run in thirty-eight games, and it would be his last.

———

The score was tied 1–1 when Joe walked to the plate in the top of the third with two outs and no one on. The first pitch was a fastball outside, and when I saw it, I knew what would happen next. The second pitch was just like the first, hard and a foot off the plate. I wanted to stand and scream, "Look out, Joe!" but I couldn't move. As my father stood on the mound and looked in at Jerry Grote, my heart froze and I couldn't breathe. I managed to say to my mother, "He's gonna hit him."

The beanball went straight at Joe's helmet, and for a second, for a long, dreadful second that fans and writers would discuss and debate and analyze for decades to come, Joe didn't move. He lost the ball. For a reason no one, especially Joe, would ever understand or be able to explain or re-create or re-enact, he simply lost sight of the ball. He had said that he preferred to hit from the left side because he felt as though his right eye picked up the pitches faster, but at that crucial split second his eyes failed him. It could have been something beyond the center field wall. It could have been a slight shift in the lighting. He could have lost the ball as it crossed between my father's white jersey and home plate. He could have been distracted by the movements of Felix Millan, the second baseman. No one would ever know because Joe would never remember.

The sound of a leather baseball hitting a hard plastic batting helmet is unmistakable. I had heard it several times in my games, including twice when I had unintentionally hit batters. I had heard it a month before at Shea when Bud Harrelson got beaned. I had heard it the summer before at a minor-league game I attended with Tom Sabbatini and

his father. It is not a sharp bang but
more like the striking of a dull object on
a hard surface. It's frightening enough,
but there is also the immediate belief
that the helmet has prevented a serious
injury.

It was not the sound of Joe being hit.
What we heard was the sickening thud
of the baseball cracking into flesh and
bone. For those of us in the crowd close
enough to hear it, the sound would never
be forgotten.

I can, and do, still hear it today.

The ball made contact at the corner
of his right eye. It knocked his helmet
off as he fell backward. He caught himself with his hands behind him, on the
ground, and paused for a second before passing out.

There are so many scrambled images
of what happened next. The crowd was
stunned. There were gasps and a lot of
"Oh my Gods!" The home plate umpire
was waving for help. Jerry Grote was
standing helplessly over Joe. The Cubs
bench was ready to explode; several
players were out of the dugout, screaming and cursing at Warren Tracey. The

Cubs fans were booing loudly. The Mets fans were silent. My father walked slowly to a spot behind the mound, took off his glove, put both hands on his hips, and stared at home plate. I hated him.

As the trainers hovered over Joe and we waited, I closed my eyes and prayed that he would get up. Shake it off. Trot down to first. Then at some point charge the mound and bloody my father's face, just like Dutch Patton's. My mother stared at the field in disbelief, then looked down at me. My eyes were wet.

Minutes passed, and Joe was not getting up. We could see his cleats and uniform from the knees down, and at one point his heels appeared to be twitching, as if his body were in a seizure. The Cubs fans began throwing debris, and security guards scurried onto the field. Jerry Grote walked past the mound and stood next to his pitcher. I watched my father closely and at one point saw something that did not surprise me. With Joe flat on his back, unconscious, seriously injured, and convulsing, I saw my father smile.

A gate opened in right field, and an ambulance appeared. It stopped near home plate, a stretcher was removed, and suddenly the doctors, medics, and trainers were much more agitated. Whatever Joe's condition was, it was getting worse. They quickly loaded him into the ambulance, and it sped away. All fifty-five thousand fans stood and applauded, though Joe heard nothing.

———

During the break, the Cubs had time to review their options. Warren Tracey had fanned on three straight pitches to make the final out in the bottom of the second, so he would not bat again until the fifth inning. With Ferguson Jenkins pitching for the Cubs, no one in the world of baseball doubted for a second that my father was about to get beaned. Retaliation would be swift and, hopefully, at least for the Cubs, brutal and painful. However, Yogi Berra might decide to pull Tracey for a reliever, thus preventing the payback. The Cubs could also retaliate in the bottom of the third by knocking down one or two of the Mets hitters. This would probably result in a free-for-all, which was exactly what the Cubs wanted as they watched their fallen star ride away in the ambulance. The problem with a brawl was that their target would be safely tucked away in the dugout. What the Cubs wanted was the head of Warren Tracey, and the manager, Whitey Lockman, devised the perfect solution. To pinch run for Joe, Lockman inserted a part-time player named Razor Ruffin, a tough black kid from the Memphis projects, which he escaped by playing football and baseball at Michigan State. He was built like a fireplug and could run like a deer, but as the Cubs were learning, he struggled with left-handed pitching. He entered the game and took his time stretching at first base.

The beaning of Joe Castle caused a thirty-minute delay in the game, and after he was gone, the umpire allowed Warren Tracey a few warm-up throws. The stadium was subdued. The Mets fans were uneasy, and the Cubs fans were exhausted from screaming and booing. Billy Williams stepped to the plate and dug in from the left side. Williams, a future Hall of Famer, was an easygoing type, but at that moment any pitch even close to his head would start trouble. Razor Ruffin took a lead but stayed close to the bag. He was in the game to fight, not steal. Tracey's first two pitches were far outside. He had lost his rhythm and was throwing, not pitching. With the count 2 and 2, Williams hit a lazy pop fly to center, an easy third out. When it was obvious the ball would be caught by Don Hahn, Razor Ruffin broke for the mound. As Warren Tracey watched the fly ball, Ruffin slammed into the back of his knees and knocked him halfway to third base. Ruffin then pounced on him with both fists and began flailing away. The Cubs, who of course knew the plan, launched a full assault and engulfed Tracey and Jerry Grote. The rest of the Mets were a few steps behind, but within seconds one of baseball's ugliest incidents was under way. Fistfights spun off as old scores

were settled. Bodies hit the turf as four
dozen great athletes kicked and punched
and tried to kill each other with their
bare hands. At the bottom of the pile,
Razor Ruffin and Warren Tracey were
still locked up, choking, gouging, trying
to break bones and draw blood. The
umpires were hapless in their efforts to
separate the teams. Security guards
poured onto the field. Normally, the
coaches would try to unlock their players, but not with this brawl. As it continued, the fans went wild, and Shea Stadium seemed on the verge of a riot.
Bedlam reigned until a few of the veterans for both teams—Ron Santo, Rusty
Staub, Billy Williams, and Tom Seaver—
succeeded in pulling their teammates
away from the action. When the pile was
uncovered, Warren Tracey bounced up
with a bloody nose and pointed his finger at one of the Cubs. The umpires
shoved him away, and two of his teammates dragged him toward the dugout.
He was cursing, shouting, and bleeding
until he disappeared. Order was finally
restored. Both managers were ejected,

along with Tracey, Ruffin, and six of their teammates.

———

By the time the game resumed, I was too stunned to think clearly. I had witnessed a nightmare—the gruesome beaning of Joe Castle, followed by the emotional shock of watching my father get pummeled by an entire team. My mother was fed up too. "I'd like to leave now," she whispered. "Me too," I said.

We rode the train home without a word. I went to my room and crawled into the bed. I did not turn on the television, though I was desperate for news about Joe. I was determined not to fall asleep because I had to know if my father came home that night. I doubted he would, and I was right. Shortly before midnight, the phone rang and my mother answered it. A male voice threatened to kill Warren Tracey and burn down our house in the process. My mother called the police, and at 2:00 a.m. my mother and I were chatting with an officer at the kitchen table.

It was the first of many threatening

calls. For the next few months we lived in fear, and of course my father was rarely home to protect us.

At the age of eleven, I wanted to change my name.

13

The mosquitoes find us, and we retreat from the porch. Fay serves strawberries and cream, with some strange herbal tea, in the cluttered library. From ceiling to floor, the walls are covered with rows of books, and there are neat stacks around an old desk. Indeed, there are books all over the house, most covered with dust and packed on sagging shelves, much like an old secondhand bookshop. The Rooks are well-read and thoroughly engaging as conversationalists. I have talked enough and want to listen for a while.

"We were listening to the game on the porch, weren't we, Fay?" Clarence asks.

"Yes, around front. I'll never forget it." As the evening progresses, I realize Fay knows almost as much about the game as Clarence. "Very sad."

"Vince Lloyd and Lou Boudreau seemed to know immediately that Joe was not getting up. Lou flat out called it a beanball, a payback since Joe had homered the first time up. As we waited and waited, they filled in the gap with some research. Warren Tracey had led the National League in hit batsmen in 1972 and was tied for the lead in 1973. Lou called him a headhunter, among other things. Both agreed that Joe seemed to freeze when the pitch was released. You could tell from their tone that the situation was pretty grim."

"Has Joe ever talked about it around here?" I ask. "Not on the record, but maybe to his friends or even his brothers?"

"Not to my knowledge," Clarence replies. "A few years later, a reporter from Little Rock—was it the *Democrat* or the *Gazette*, Fay?"

"I think it was the *Gazette*," she says. "It's in one of the notebooks."

"But this guy showed up and managed to get an audience with Charlie and Red. He quizzed them about how Joe was doing these days, and so on. He also asked about the beaning, and they said that Joe simply doesn't remember it. That's the only time I can recall the family talking about it. Must've been twenty years ago."

"Is there brain damage?" I ask.

Clarence and Fay look at each other, and it is obvious there are things not to be discussed in my presence. "I don't think so," he says, finally, "but he's not a hundred percent."

Fay says, "Clarence is one of the few townsfolk Joe will speak to. Not talk to, as in a conversation, but he has always liked Clarence and will at least acknowledge his presence."

"I'm not sure anyone other than his mother really knows what goes on inside his head," Clarence says.

"And he lives with her?"

"Yes, three blocks away."

It is almost 10:00 p.m., and Fay is

ready for bed. She gathers the dishes, gives me instructions on where to sleep, and says good night. As soon as she is gone, Clarence says, "I need a little digestif, you?"

As far as I can tell, Clarence is cold sober. He did not finish his last lemon gin over dinner and shows no sign of being tipsy. Same for me—my last sip of alcohol (and the last sip of lemon gin in my lifetime) was two hours earlier. My clock is running on mountain time, one hour behind Arkansas, so I am not quite ready for bed. And I want to listen to Clarence. "Such as?" I ask.

He is already on his feet, lumbering out of the room. "Ozark peach brandy," he says and disappears.

It is a clear liquid with a slight amber tint. He pours it from an ominous-looking jug into two small shot-like glasses. When he sits down, we touch glasses and he says, "Cheers. Now, be careful. You need to sip it very slowly at first."

I do. A blowtorch could not be hotter on my lips and tongue. I keep a game face and manage to choke it down, with flames scorching my esophagus until

the last drop hits my unsuspecting stomach. He watches me carefully, waiting
for some comical reaction, and when I
keep my composure, he says, "Not bad,
huh?"

"What is it—gasoline?"

"It's a local product made by one of
our better distillers."

"And untaxed, I presume?"

"Highly untaxed and illegal as hell."
He takes another sip.

"I thought moonshine causes blind-
ness and liver damage."

"It can, but you gotta know your
source. This is good stuff, some of the
best—light, tasty, virtually harmless."

Harmless? My toes are burning. As
the child of a violent alcoholic, I have
never been attracted to the drinking life,
and after an evening of lemon gin and
moonshine whiskey I realize how wise I
have been.

"The second sip is easier, and the
third is the best," he says. I take an even
smaller sip, and it burns less, probably
because of the scar tissue left behind
by the first.

"Tell me, Paul, how did you know your

father was going to bean Joe?" he asks, reaching for his pipe and tobacco pouch.

"That's a long story," I say, trying to find my tongue.

He smiles and spreads his arms. "We have all night. I usually read until midnight and sleep till eight."

I take a third sip and actually get a slight taste of peach flavoring. "He was of the old school. If a batter hits a home run, then the batter wins the duel. His reward is obvious; he gets nothing more. It's a sin to insult the pitcher by showing off in any way. Standing at the plate and admiring the drive; flipping the bat; loafing around the bases to soak up the attention; and heaven forbid any show of self-gratification or emotion. No sir. The batter wins, and he circles the bases quickly and gets to the dugout. Otherwise, he pays for it. If a batter does anything to show off, then the pitcher has the right to knock him down. That was straight from the old code, and my father swore by it."

"That might not work in today's game," Clarence says, blowing a cloud of smoke.

"I wouldn't know, Clarence. I haven't watched a game in thirty years."

"So, did Joe do something to show up Warren Tracey? You were there. Vince Lloyd and Lou Boudreau said repeatedly that Joe did nothing wrong."

"Well, according to Warren's official party line, the answer is no. No, because he soon began claiming that it was an accident, he did not throw at Joe, that it was simply a pitch up that got away from him. I suspect that once it became obvious Joe was seriously injured, Warren changed his tune and started lying."

"You seem awfully certain about this."

"When I was a little boy, five or six, I decided I wanted to be a pitcher because my father was a pitcher. I was pretty good and got better as I grew up. I didn't get a lot of backyard coaching because he was seldom at home, but we lived in the same house, and some of his knowledge rubbed off on me, I guess. I was pitching once and a kid hit a home run, a real shot, and he danced and yelled all the way around the bases. My father was there, which was a rare occasion, and the next time this kid came up, my father yelled, 'Knock him down, Paul.' I was eleven years old and didn't want to throw at anyone. The kid did not get beaned. My father was furious. After the game, we had a big fight. He slapped me around the backyard, told me I would never make it as a pitcher because I was a coward, afraid to throw at hitters. He was a nasty person, Clarence."

Another sip, another puff. "And you'll see him tomorrow?"

"That's right, for the first time in several years."

"And you think you can convince him to come here, to Calico Rock?"

"I have no idea, but I'll try."

"It seems like a long shot, on both ends."

"I have a plan. It might not work, but I'm trying."

He pours some more moonshine. After a few minutes, I begin to nod off. "Does this stuff knock you out?" I ask.

"Definitely. You'll sleep like a baby."

"I'm gone. Thanks."

I go to bed in their guest room, beneath the hum and breeze of a ceiling fan, only three blocks away from the small house where Joe Castle lives with his mother. The last time I saw him he was on a stretcher being rushed off the field, away to a New York City hospital, leaving behind forever the brilliance of his game, the dreams of his fans, and the promising career that would never be.

———

Fay is consumed with her work at her easel when I say good-bye. I thank her for the hospitality, and she says the guest room is always available. I follow Clarence back to Main Street, where we park and walk to Evans Drug Store. As we enter, he says, "You might want to stick with Paul Casey, just to be safe."

No problem. I have used that alias more times than he can imagine.

The café is filled with the early morning crowd, all men, and Clarence speaks to a few as we head for a table in the rear. I manage to avoid having to introduce myself. Evidently, Clarence is a vegetarian only at home, where Fay is in charge of the menu. Away from her, he orders eggs and bacon, and I do likewise. Waiting on the food, we sip coffee and listen to the enthusiastic conversations around us. At a long table near the front window, a group of retired gentlemen are worked up over the war in Iraq. There are plenty of opinions and little regard for who else in the café might hear them.

"I assume this is a fairly conservative town, politically," I say to Clarence.

"Oh yes, but it's usually split during elections. Izard County is all white, but there are a lot of your old-time Roosevelt Democrats still around. They're known as 'drop-cord Democrats.' "

"That's a new one."

"Rural electricity, brought in by the New Deal way back."

"Why is the county all white?"

"It's historic. There was never much farming around here, so no slaves. No reason for black folks to settle here. Now I guess they prefer to go elsewhere, but we've never had a problem with the Klan, if that's what you're thinking."

"No, that's not what I was thinking."

The wall above the cash register is

covered with rows of team photos—Little League, softball, high school basketball— some current, others faded with the years. In the center is a framed cover of the August 6, 1973, edition of *Sports Illustrated*. Calico Joe, the Phenom. I look at it and smile. "I remember the day it arrived in the mail," I say.

"We all do. Probably the greatest day in the town's history."

"Do folks around here still talk about Joe?"

"Seldom. It's been thirty years, you know? I can't recall the last conversation about him."

The eggs and bacon arrive. The war wages not far away. We eat quickly, and I pay the check, cash—no credit card. I don't want anyone to see my name. Clarence decides we should take his car—a maroon Buick—because a strange vehicle with out-of-state license plates might stir suspicion. Not surprisingly, the Buick smells like stale pipe tobacco. Air-conditioning is not an option, and we make the short drive with the windows down.

The high school is a mile or so from

Main Street, in a newer section of town. I know that Calico Rock is too small for a football team, so when I see lights, I know the baseball field is close. In the distance, in center field, a man is riding a turf mower. "That's him," Clarence says.

Fall classes have yet to begin, and the lots are empty. We park near an old rodeo arena, cross a street, and approach the backstop from behind some bleachers. We climb to the top row and settle into a spot shaded by the small press box. The field is beautiful. The Bermuda grass is lush and green. Everything else is wilting under the August sun and drought, but the turf of Joe Castle Field is thick, manicured, and well irrigated. The base paths and infield dirt are meticulously groomed. The mound looks as though it has been hand sculpted. A ten-foot-wide warning track of crushed limestone circles the entire playing surface, and there is not a weed visible. Just beyond the chain-link fence in left center is a large scoreboard with JOE CASTLE FIELD across the top and

HOME OF THE PIRATES along the bottom.

Joe is on a red spiderlike mower with various cutting decks and numerous blades, a serious machine obviously built for playing surfaces. He wears a black cap with the bill pulled low and glasses. Not surprisingly, he has put on weight over the years.

"He's here every day?" I ask.

"Five days a week."

"It's the middle of August. There won't be another baseball game until, what, March?"

"Middle of March, if it's not snowing."

"So why does he cut the grass and prepare the field every day?"

"Because he wants to. It's his job."

"He's paid?"

"Oh yes. Joe came home just before Christmas of 1973. He spent two months in a hospital in New York, then the Cubs flew him to Chicago, where he spent several weeks in another hospital. Red and Charlie drove him home in time for Christmas. He was talking about playing some more, but we knew the truth. Just after the first of the year, he had the stroke, a massive one. He was at home, by himself, and by the time they got him to the hospital in Mountain Home, there was some damage. His left side is partially paralyzed. You'll see when he walks."

"Does he know we're up here?"

"Yes. He saw us park, walk over, find a seat. He knows we're talking about him. It's likely he will not get close enough to say hello, and before the day is over, either Red or Charlie, probably Charlie, will call me and want to know what I was doing here and who I had with me. I'll tell him you're my nephew from Texas, a high school baseball coach who wanted to admire our field."

"Okay. Back to the story. Why is Joe paid to take care of the field?"

"After the stroke, it was obvious he was disabled and needed a job. So the school system hired him as a custodian, full-time with health insurance and pension, and for thirty years Joe has been taken care of. He works on the field, putters around the gymnasium, and when the baseball team has a game, he sits up here in the press box and works the scoreboard."

"What a great idea."

"We take care of each other here in Calico Rock, Paul. Especially Joe."

Joe finishes a long sweeping cut, from the right field foul line to the left, then whirls around for another one. The mower is close to the outfield warning track. If the blades are actually clipping the Bermuda, I cannot detect it. The uncut portion looks as pristine as the swath he's just finished.

"What are you thinking?" Clarence asks, firing up his pipe again.

"What could have been. Where would Joe be now had it not been for the injury. How great could he have been?"

"That'll drive you crazy. I did it for years, then realized it's a waste of time. The story of Joe Castle is nothing but a great tragedy. It's difficult to accept, but after a while you try to move on."

"Is it a good idea for Warren Tracey to come here, to meet with Joe?"

A long puff, a large cloud of smoke. The temperature has to be close to ninety already, and I wonder how a person can enjoy smoking in such heat. "You know, Paul, sitting here as we are, it seems impossible that your father would show up, shake hands with Joe, and talk about their past."

"Yes, it does."

"Do you really think you can convince him to come?"

"I'm going to try, Clarence. I think I can do it."

"How?"

"Blackmail."

Joe turns for the final swipe at the outfield grass. He has yet to look in our direction.

"I don't suppose I want to get into that," Clarence says.

"No, you don't."

We watch and listen to the mower. Finally, Clarence says, "Yes, in my worthless opinion, it would mean a lot to Joe if Warren Tracey shook his hand and offered his apology. The two have never spoken, never met since that night. It strikes me as a good idea. But how in hell can you pull it off?"

"It's a long shot, Clarence. But I need your help. I want you to speak to his

brothers and clear it on this end. Otherwise, I'm wasting my time."

Joe parks in foul territory outside the
left field line and turns off the mower.
He swings his right leg over, braces himself, and hops down. He grabs a cane
and shuffles toward a storage shed. He
walks with a pronounced limp, with his
left foot dragging behind, his right foot
advancing in stutter steps, his shoulders
dipping as he slowly moves forward.

"That poor guy," I say, and a part of
me feels like crying. That beautiful young
kid who could fly from home to first in
under four seconds, who stole second
and third back-to-back seven times in
thirty-eight games, who turned lazy singles into thrilling doubles, that magnifi-
cent athlete with greatness emanating
from every part of his game, has been
reduced to a crippled custodian who
mows grass that does not need mow-
ing. Just the thought of it—when Joe
was thirty years old and should have
been in the prime of a great career, he
was, instead, doing exactly what he is
doing now.

"Very sad," Clarence adds. Joe disappears into the storage shed. "We probably won't see him again. I guess we should leave."

———

As we return to Main Street, Clarence agrees to approach Charlie and Red and explore the idea of a meeting. I repeat the obvious: Warren does not have long to live. There is no time to waste.

We stop by the *Calico Rock Record*, where I find a cup of coffee. It takes a while to say good-bye. We have enjoyed our time together and sincerely hope we meet again soon. Leaving the town, I have no idea if I will ever return.

Four hours later, I am in Memphis. I fly through Atlanta on my way to Tampa, where I rent another car and drive east, toward Winter Haven.

14

Long after the police officer left, my mother and I sat in the den and watched westerns. The doors were bolted; the shades were drawn; every light in the house was on; the officer promised to patrol our street; and we were still afraid. Perhaps we should have dismissed the call as a prank by an irate Cubs fan who found our number in the phone book, but it felt much more serious than that. We had never received such a threat, and given the trauma and emotions of the night, we were unable to shrug it off and go to sleep.

During a commercial, my mother asked, "How did you know he was going to hit Joe Castle?" She was on one end of the sofa, I was on the other, both of us were still dressed.

"Because that's the way he plays baseball," I replied.

"Why do they allow beanballs?"

"I don't know. I've never heard a good reason."

"Such a stupid sport," she said.

I didn't argue. We were also afraid that Warren might stagger home and cause trouble. He had been forced off the field with a bloody nose, so he wasn't badly injured in the brawl. But if he wasn't home by 3:00 a.m., he wasn't coming home. He was probably in a bar, showing off his bruises, bragging about his skills as a beanball artist, and no doubt taking credit for the Mets win.

I dozed off, but at 6:00 a.m. my mother nudged me and said, "Here's the news." Channel 4 out of Manhattan began the day at 6:00 a.m. with news, weather, and sports, and they didn't waste time getting to the story. "A wild night at Shea," the reporter gushed as the footage rolled. From a camera somewhere near the Mets dugout, the tape showed the beanball and Joe going down. Again, in slow motion, and again as the reporter described it in detail. He said that Joe was in serious condition at Mount Sinai Hospital in Manhattan.

At least he was alive.

Next up was the brawl, and just as in real time it seemed to go on forever. Having been an eyewitness, I had seen enough. The entire episode made me sick and depressed, and as I realized later, it would turn me against the sport.

When the sun was up, I walked to the end of the driveway and retrieved the *New York Times*. I glanced up and down the street to make sure everything was safe but at the time did not realize I would be looking over my shoulder for many months to come.

My mother sipped coffee and flipped through section A. I, of course, read every word about the game and all of its related issues. The front page of the sports section had two large photos. The first was Joe on the ground sec-

onds after being hit and before the trainers crowded around him. The second
was a beautiful shot of Razor Ruffin flat-
tening my father with a bruising tackle.
Ruffin had no comment after the game,
nor did Warren Tracey, Yogi Berra,
Whitey Lockman, or any other player or
coach. There was little doubt, though,
that the fighting was far from over. The
two teams squared off again at 2:00
p.m. that afternoon. The doctors at
Mount Sinai weren't saying much, but
Joe was unconscious and in serious
condition.

The phone rang, and we both stared
at it for a second. I was closer, so I
slowly lifted the receiver. "Hello."

An agitated voice yelled, "Warren
Tracey is a dead man!"

My mother quickly unplugged the
phones.

The Chicago newspapers were out-
raged. "Beaned!" screamed the headline in the *Sun-Times*, just above a photo
of Joe Castle on the ground, his helmet
nearby. The *Tribune* was somewhat

more restrained. Its headline read, "Mets Find Way to Stop Castle."

Mid-morning Saturday, Commissioner Bowie Kuhn met with his executives in the offices of Major League Baseball in New York City. After reviewing the footage and talking to eyewitnesses, he suspended Razor Ruffin and Whitey Lockman for ten games, Warren Tracey for five, and eight other players for three games each. His office issued a banal statement wishing Joe Castle a speedy recovery.

Shea was sold out again for the Saturday game, with many more Cubs fans there and looking for trouble. A smoke bomb landed near home plate just after the first pitch was thrown by Tom Seaver. The game was delayed for fifteen minutes while the air cleared. The Mets fans booed, the Cubs fans cursed, the atmosphere in the park was tense. Security was beefed up considerably, and uniformed policemen stood almost shoulder to shoulder along the warning track. Joe had been hit by the third pitch thrown to the third batter in the third inning, and with perfect coordination a wave of smoke bombs rained down on the field as Tom Seaver threw the third pitch to Burt Hooton, the Cubs starter, in the top of the third inning. Fights broke out as Mets fans attacked the bombers. Arrests were made. The game was delayed for half an hour as warnings blared from the PA announcer. An ugly situation was getting worse.

I tried to watch the game but could not. I wanted to leave the house and hide at the Sabbatinis' for a few hours, or a few days, but then my mother would have been by herself. So I stayed in my room, turned the radio on and off, and killed time.

When the Mets were in town and my father was home, I usually waited a couple of days before clipping articles from the sports page for my scrapbooks. But I was bored, and he wasn't home, and I frankly did not care what he thought. Sitting at the kitchen table, I carefully cut out the stories from the *Times*, then went to my closet, where I kept a dozen scrapbooks, photo albums, and card collections. I maintained these in a meticulous order, and to my knowledge no one ever touched them but me. Because of the avalanche of stories and photos of Joe Castle and his historic debut, I had reassembled all of his material into his very own scrapbook. The only other players to be so honored were Tom Seaver, Willie Mays, Hank Aaron, and Catfish Hunter. The rest of the scrapbooks were collections of memorabilia, articles, and photos dedicated to entire teams—the 1973 Mets, the 1972 Mets, the Big Red Machine, the 1972 Oakland A's, and so on. Two years earlier, I had opened a scrapbook dedicated to my father, but there simply was not enough material to sustain it.

My Joe Castle scrapbook was missing. I searched every inch of my closet and my room, and when I was certain it was not there, I stretched out on my bed and stared at the ceiling. Jill was away at camp, and besides, she wouldn't touch anything remotely related to baseball. Nor would my mother.

Our home had a basement with a small washroom, an even smaller utility room, and a large game room with a television and a pool table. From the game room, there was a door that led to the backyard. Coming home at all hours of the early morning, my father often crept into the game room and passed out on the narrow sofa. Sometimes he slept there when my parents were fighting. Sometimes they fought there, away from Jill and me. Often, on the days when he pitched, he would spend hours down there, alone, with the shades pulled and lights off, lost in his own world. He considered the game room to be his own private little territory, and that was fine with the rest of us. If he wanted it for himself, we were happy to stay away.

I eased down the stairs, flipping on lights. In the game room, I found my scrapbook on an end table next to the sofa. It was open to the eight-by-ten photograph, inscribed to me, "To Paul Tracey, with best wishes, Joe Castle."

Next to the scrapbook was an orange Mets stadium cup, his cup, the only cup from which he would drink his banana milk shake precisely six hours before his first pitch. He had once flown into a rage and broken dishes in the kitchen when he couldn't find the damned cup.

I froze when I realized what I had discovered. It was like walking into a crime scene and having a delayed reaction as the truth settled in. Alone and in the semidarkness, the criminal had quietly plotted his actions, then inadvertently left behind the evidence.

I backed away and went to find my mother.

We were both rattled, frightened, and tired, and we decided to leave. We packed our bags quickly, locked the house, and drove to Hagerstown, Maryland, to stay with her parents for a few days. Warren could have the house and the death threats and all the baggage and debris he so richly deserved. I didn't realize it at the time, and I'm not sure my mother did either, but it was our first big step toward separation.

The Mets won the second game of the series that Saturday, and did so without having to fight for it. Two pitchers were ejected for throwing at batters, and both teams were itching for another brawl. But with so many players suspended, the issue of winning games became more important than winning beanball wars.

Baseball waited for Joe to wake up, to snap out of it, put some ice on his wounds, return to the stadium, and continue to dazzle and set records, but as of Sunday morning he was still in a coma.

The Mets won Sunday, and on Monday night completed a four-game sweep. The Cubs had roared into New York with a ten-game lead, and they limped out of town reeling and already feeling the pressure of another late-season collapse. They had won twenty-eight of the thirty-eight games in which Joe had played, but they were obviously a different team without him.

On August 30, Warren Tracey started at Shea against the Pirates. He gave up a single to the leadoff hitter, then walked the next two. With the bases loaded, he hit Willie Stargell in the ribs. It was not intentional, but nonetheless Stargell didn't appreciate being hit, especially by a pitcher who was by then the most notorious headhunter in the game. He said something to my father as he slowly walked to first base, and for a moment things were tense. The umpires, on high alert, jumped in and prevented trouble. His next pitch was a fastball down the middle, and Richie Hebner hit it four hundred feet for a grand slam. By the time Yogi could get him out of the game, the Pirates were up 7–0 with no outs.

Four days later, on September 3, Labor Day, my father walked to the mound at Busch Stadium in St. Louis and was met with a thunderous round of boos and hisses. He lasted two innings, walked four, struck out none, hit no one, gave up five runs, and was rapidly pitching himself out of the rotation. The New York sportswriters were howling for his replacement.

With Joe Castle still unconscious in a New York hospital, Warren Tracey was hated everywhere he went. His name was toxic. His pitching was a disaster. His teammates were winning, but they were also tired of the distractions he brought to the game. It was obvious he wasn't worth the trouble he was causing.

15

After his first two or three wives, Warren began marrying for money instead of looks and lust. One of his later ones, Florence, died from heatstroke and left him with a nice home and some cash in the bank. He isn't rich, but comfortable enough to avoid work and spend his days at the club playing gin rummy and golf and drinking. When he was about fifty-five, roughly ten years ago, his then wife, Karen, I believe, convinced him to sober up and stop smoking. To his credit, he did, though the damage to his body had been done. Poor Karen. She

soon realized he was far more agree-
able on the sauce than off. They divorced, and, never solo for long, he took
up with Agnes, the current wife.

They live in one of those typical Florida gated communities, with rows of
low-slung modern houses tucked along
fairways and ponds and around putting
greens. Everyone is over sixty and drives
a golf cart.

On the subject of golf. As soon as his
baseball career ended, Warren plunged
headlong into what he hoped would be
a new career on the tour. He hooked up
with a pro somewhere near Sarasota
and played and practiced for hours every day. He was thirty-five and the odds
were against him, but he felt as though
he had nothing to lose. He qualified for
the Citrus Circuit, a low-budget south
Florida tour, sort of like Class B minor-
league baseball. He won his second
tournament and got his name in the fine
print of the *Miami Herald*. Someone saw
it. That someone told others, and a
rough plan came together. At the next
tournament, just as Warren was about
to hit his first tee shot, a pack of Cubs

diehards began jeering and cursing him. He stepped away, exchanged words, and waited for an official to intervene. Such tournaments, though, are not heavily secured or supervised, and the hooligans refused to go away. When his first tee shot landed in a small lake, the Cubs fans cheered and howled. They followed him from hole to hole on the front nine, and he fell to pieces.

The concentration of a golfer is fragile—witness the strict rules regarding fan behavior at a PGA event. Warren, though, was far from the PGA, and the Citrus Circuit could do little to control what few fans showed up. They stalked Warren Tracey, and wherever he played, they waited in ambush. In one tournament, he birdied the first three holes, in silence, then was verbally assaulted by several large, belligerent young men as he approached the tee box on number four. His scores continued to rise, along with his blood pressure, and when he shot an 88 in the second round of his fifth tournament, he quit.

Evidently, there are a lot of Cubs fans in Florida, and over the years Warren had a number of run-ins with them on golf courses. He also had fights in bars, stores, and airports, and for a long time he traded in cash and avoided credit cards. He once got screwed out of $40,000 in a condo deal by two men who were Cubs fans and deliberately suckered him into the transaction. The surname Tracey is not that common, and for years after the beaning it meant trouble for Warren.

———

The ancient security guard clears me through the gate. It is early evening, and couples are biking and walking for exercise along the footpaths next to the winding street. The golf course is deserted. Everything is green and well-groomed.

According to my research, the home was appraised at $650,000 and had been purchased by Warren and Agnes five years earlier. I didn't keep records, but it must be the fifteenth place he has lived in Florida in the past thirty years. I suppose Warren is the restless type; he tires quickly of wives and homes.

I have not seen him in four years. Sara and I did the obligatory Disney World trip with the girls, and for some reason I thought it was important for the kids to at least meet their paternal grandfather. What a disaster. He did not want us in his home, nor did he want us to meet Agnes. So we met for lunch at a chain restaurant—Wink's Waffles—not far from his gated community, and he struggled to be civil. He had not met my children before, and Warren in the role of grandfather was a pathetic sight. He was a stranger to the girls, to Sara, and to me as well, and he could not have been more uncomfortable.

Sara's parents live in Pueblo, Colorado, and we see them several times a year. They adore their granddaughters and are as involved in their lives as possible. So the girls had a clear idea of what a grandfather should be. Warren, though, completely baffled them. He was unsure of their names, thoroughly uninterested in small talk, and showed no warmth whatsoever because he had neither the desire nor the ability, and when he glanced at his watch thirty minutes into the little family reunion, it was noticed by all of us.

Afterward, I promised Sara and the girls that they would never again be subjected to my father. I knew they approved of this decision. Later, once we were home, the girls told their mother that they felt sorry for me. They could not comprehend how a nice guy like their dad could have such a lousy father.

Parked on the cobblestoned driveway is a Mercedes that is at least fifteen years old. I ring the doorbell, and Agnes eventually answers. This is our first face-to-face meeting. It will be brief. Neither she nor I want to spend ten seconds together. She is the latest victim in a long, sad list of vulnerable and desperate women who, out of loneliness or some other unfathomable reason, agreed to marry Warren Tracey. As I follow her through the foyer, I wonder how many husbands she has been through, but I really don't care.

Warren is in the den watching television, some breed of delicate little lapdog on the sofa next to him. He rises quickly, manages a smile, and offers a hand. As I shake it, I am impressed by his appearance. His skin is pale, his movements slow, but for a dying man he looks remarkably healthy. He mutes the television but does not turn it off. Nothing he does, regardless of how rude, surprises me. I back into a chair, while Agnes sits on the sofa next to the dog. I'll get rid of her in a minute.

We kill some time talking about his surgery, and I feign interest. Next, it's the chemotherapy, which will start in a week. "I'm gonna beat this thing, Paul," he says, a well-rehearsed line delivered with no conviction. He seems to think I care. He seems to believe I have traveled from New Mexico to Florida because I am concerned about him. There is no doubt in my mind that if I were hospitalized and on my deathbed, Warren Tracey would find an excuse not to show up. Why, then, does he think I am interested in his chemo?

Why? Over the years, I've learned the answer. He's special. He played the game. Maybe he didn't put up Hall of Fame numbers, but he was still one of the elite who made it to the big stage. His entire life has been lived in his own little self-absorbed, narcissistic world where he is a cut above the rest.

I feed him quarters and keep him talking. How long will the chemotherapy last? What do the doctors really think? I know a guy whose uncle lived fifteen years with pancreatic cancer. Is more surgery a possibility?

He does not ask about my wife, my daughters, his daughter, or her children. As usual, it's all about Warren.

Agnes, who's a little on the chunky side and easily as old as Warren, just sits there rubbing the dog and grinning goofily at Warren, as if his narratives are witty and original. It doesn't take much to amuse Agnes, I decide after ten minutes. I wonder if it has crossed her mind that in virtually all polite circles she, as the hostess, is expected to offer me something to drink.

I look at her and say, "Say, Agnes, I have a few things I need to discuss with Warren in private. You know, family stuff, rather personal. Could the two of us have a few minutes?"

She does not like this at all, but Warren smiles and nods his head at the
door. She huffs out of the den, closing
the door behind her. I reach over, take
the remote, turn off the television, sit
back down, and say, "Guess who I saw
this morning, Warren?"

"How should I know?"

"Always the smart-ass, right?"

"Always, yes."

"Joe Castle, that's who. I was in Calico Rock yesterday afternoon and last
night, and this morning I saw Joe."

"I suppose you were just passing
through."

"No, not at all. I went there for the
purpose of seeing him."

His shoulders sag a little as the air
gets heavier. I am staring at him, but he
has found something on the floor to hold
his gaze. A minute passes, then another.
He finally grunts and says, "Something
you want to say?"

I move closer to him and sit on the
edge of the coffee table. Two feet away,
I realize how little sympathy I have for
this dying old man. There is far more
anger than pity, but I promised myself I

would not visit our past. "I want you to go see Joe, Warren. Now, before it's too late, before you pass away, before he passes away. There will never be another time like now. Go, sit down with him, offer a hand, offer the truth, offer an apology, at least attempt to close this story."

He frowns as if in severe pain. He looks at me as his mouth falls open, and for a while he cannot speak.

"I'm serious, Warren. You have lied for thirty years about what happened, but you and I both know the truth. For once in your miserable life, stand up and admit you're wrong, apologize. You've never reached out to him. You would never face him. You would never face the truth, quite the opposite. You've lied and lied and lied until you probably believe your own lies. Stop the lying, tell Joe the truth, and tell him you're sorry."

"You got a lot of guts coming here with this crap," he snarls.

"I have far more guts than you, old man. If you had a backbone, you would go see him. I'll go with you. We'll make the journey together, and when it's over, you'll feel a lot better about yourself."

"Aren't you the wise one?"

"I am, on this matter anyway."

His pale face has reddened with anger, but he holds his tongue. Another minute passes. "What did you say to him?" he asks.

"Nothing. We didn't speak. I saw him from a distance. He walks with a bad limp, and a cane, thanks to you."

"I did not intend to hit him."

I raise both hands and laugh. "Here we go again. The biggest lie in the history of organized baseball, and what's worse, everyone knows it's a lie, including both of us."

"Get out of my house!"

"I will in a minute. Let's face the truth, Warren. You won't make it to Christmas. The odds are heavily against you. When you die, those who know you are not going to say things like: 'Good ole Warren, he loved his kids.' Or, 'Good ole Warren, what a generous soul.' Or, 'Warren truly loved his wives.' Nothing like that, Warren, because it doesn't fit. The one thing that will be mentioned in your obituary, if you have one at all, is the fact that you threw the most famous beanball in the history of the game. And in doing so, you deliberately destroyed one of the most promising careers of all time. That's what they're gonna say, Warren, and you can't do a thing about it."

"Please leave."

"I'll be happy to leave, Warren, just let me finish. You can never undo the misery you created—the neglected kids, the tormented son, the abused wife, the alcoholism, the philandering, the long trail of debris you've left behind. Can't fix it, Warren, even if you are so inclined, which I'm sure you are not. But there is one person you can reach out to and perhaps make his life a little brighter. Do it, Warren. Do it for Joe. Do it for yourself. Do it for me."

"You've lost your mind."

I reach into my jacket and remove some folded papers. "I want you to read this, Warren. It's titled 'The Beaning of Joe Castle' by Paul Tracey, son of Warren. I wrote it many years ago, and I've revised it a thousand times. Every word is true. My plans are to get it published as soon as possible after your death. I'll start with *Sports Illustrated*, *Baseball Monthly*, the newspapers in Chicago, not sure after that, but I'll bet somebody will want to print it. I don't want a dime. I want the truth to be known." I drop the papers onto his lap. "The only way to prevent this from being published is to go with me to Calico Rock and see Joe."

"Blackmail?"

"You got it, Warren. Old-fashioned blackmail, but for a good reason."

I toss a business card onto the sofa and say, "I'm at the Best Western down the road. If you want to talk, I'll meet you at your favorite spot, Wink's Waffles, at nine in the morning."

He was scratching his forehead when I left the room. I did not see Agnes on the way out.

———

I check into the Best Western, call home and chat with Sara, then head downstairs to find something to eat. The restaurant is empty and uninviting, but there are a few salesmen swapping stories over drinks in a lounge. I choose a table, order a sandwich and a glass of tea, and notice a television in a corner. The Cubs are playing the Mets with the sound on mute. I stare at it, the first baseball game I've watched in thirty years.

16

On September 8, 1973, Warren Tracey started against the Padres in San Diego. He walked two in the first inning but got out of trouble with a bases-loaded double play. He walked two more in the second, then gave up back-to-back doubles. On the air, Ralph Kiner referred to his pitching as "batting practice." By the time Yogi Berra pulled him, the Padres had a five-run lead and two runners on, and the Mets, who had won eight of their last ten, were in trouble.

In his last three starts, Warren had completed just three innings, given up seventeen runs on twelve hits, walked thirteen, and had an ERA that approached triple figures. Since hitting Castle, he had lost his ability to throw inside, and every hitter in the National League knew it. The New York sportswriters and fans were screaming for his head, and it was obvious the Mets had to do something. The team was winning, with the exception of Warren, and there was open speculation about who would replace him in the rotation.

And there was more pressure. On September 15, the Mets were scheduled to arrive in Chicago for a three-game series, and there was an excellent chance that the sight of Warren Tracey on the field at Wrigley would lead to bloodshed. The death threats were pouring in—to the Mets home office, in anonymous letters to the editors, to the homes of some of the Mets players. The Chicago sportswriters were speculating about how dangerous Wrigley would be if the Mets were foolish enough to put Tracey on the mound. Commissioner Bowie Kuhn was watching the situation closely.

On September 14, three weeks after the beaning, the Mets released Warren Tracey.

Of course, my father did not call home with the news that he had been cut from the roster. That would have required some maturity and courage on his part. The Mets were in L.A., and as I tuned in for the pregame show, I heard Lindsey Nelson and Ralph Kiner talking about the decision by the Mets front office to get rid of Warren Tracey. He had pitched himself out of a job, and they spent some time recapping his season and career. A month earlier, he had a record of seven and seven and was pitching effectively. But since the Castle incident, he had been a disaster.

I could hear the relief in the voices of Nelson and Kiner. No one traveling with the Mets wanted to go into Wrigley the following day with Warren Tracey around.

My mother was playing tennis at a club a few blocks away. I decided that she should hear the news that her husband was suddenly out of work, and the sooner the better. I rode my bike over, watched her play from a distance, and when she finished, I caught her as she was leaving the court. She took it hard. Not only was he cut from the team, but at thirty-four his career was surely over. I had no idea how much money they had saved, if any, though my mother kept a pretty tight budget. And now that he had nothing to do, he would spend more time at home, a prospect that none of us looked forward to.

Our little world was unraveling. My father was out of work and over the hill. He was drinking more, staying out more, and fighting more with my mother, who was dropping hints about a new life, one without him. We had changed our phone number twice because of the anonymous calls and now had a private number. It was not unusual to see a police car parked in front of our home. We were frightened.

The Cubs won two of the three games against the Mets. There were no fights, no beanballs, and no ejections. When the series began, the teams were tied for first in the National League East, and with fifteen games to go, no one could afford another suspension or injury.

Without Joe in the lineup, the Cubs had won eleven and lost thirteen. Their ten-game lead three weeks earlier had been reduced to one. They were sinking, Chicago style, while the Mets were winning. To Cubs fans, the beaning of Joe Castle had been a deliberate attack planned by the Mets to get him off the field so their team would falter. In Warren Tracey, the Mets had the perfect attack dog—a journeyman headhunter who could do the dirty work and then get thrown out with the trash. Seaver, Koosman, and Matlack could stay above it all.

This was not just idle chatter from drunks in a bar. Many of Chicago's sportswriters were now conspiracy theorists and fanning these flames.

There was still a fervent, though fading, dream that Joe would snap out of his coma, hop off the bed, hustle out of the hospital, and take up where he left off. But with each passing day, the sad reality settled in a bit deeper. Wait till next year, the Cubs were famous for saying, but now they meant it. Wait till next year, when Joe's back and he's a year older and more experienced. Just wait.

———

On September 18, the day after the series ended and the Mets moved on to Montreal, Joe Castle woke up and spoke to a nurse. This was reported on the local station, and my mother heard it first. She told me, and I rode over to Tom Sabbatini's to discuss this exciting news. Mr. Sabbatini knew what I was going through, and he offered to take us to the hospital the following Saturday.

After school the next day, I went to the library and read the coverage in the *Tribune* and *Sun-Times*. Joe was still in serious condition, but at least he was awake, talking, and eating. Red was by his side and agreed to allow a reporter from the *Tribune* inside the room for ten minutes. The reporter asked Joe how he felt, and his response was, "I have felt much better." He was described as sedated, groggy, and not always responsive to questions. There was a photograph, a heartbreaking picture of Joe Castle with his head wrapped in thick gauze, much like a casualty from combat. His right eye was covered too. The eye was of grave concern to his doctors.

Mount Sinai had been deluged with cards, flowers, gifts, and visitors wanting to see Joe. A temporary shrine had been set up in a wide, open foyer on the ground floor. In the center, there was a large photo of Joe—the same one from the cover of *Sports Illustrated*—and to each side were long, wide panels of corkboard. Hundreds of fans had tacked on notes, cards, and letters to Joe. At the foot of the panels were cardboard boxes filled with flowers, chocolates, and other gifts.

Tom and I wrote letters, though we didn't share them before they were sealed in envelopes. In an effort to get Joe's attention, my letter began with "Dear Joe: I am Paul Tracey, Warren's son. I am so sorry for what my father did." I went on to gush about how closely

I had followed his career, how great I thought he was, and how badly I wanted him to get better and return to the field.

Saturday morning, we took the train into the city. It was a beautiful fall day; the leaves were turning and blowing in the breeze as we strolled through Central Park. When we entered the hospital from Fifth Avenue, a hand-painted sign read JOE CASTLE WALL, and an arrow pointed to the left. We found the wall and tacked our letters side by side as close to his photo as possible. A volunteer explained that the letters, cards, and gifts were collected every two or three days and would be given to Mr. Castle at some convenient time in the future. She thanked us for coming.

"Where is he?" I asked.

She looked up and said, "Fourth floor, but I'm afraid you can't go there."

"How's he doing today?"

"I've heard he's improving," she said, and she was right. According to the newspapers, he was slowly making progress, but a dramatic comeback seemed doubtful. We hung around for a few minutes, looking at the assortment

of letters, cards, and gifts. I glanced up
and down the wide corridors in the distance, all busy with the typical hospital
foot traffic. I was tempted to drift away,
find the elevators, and somehow make
my way to the fourth floor, where I could
cleverly sneak into Joe's room for a private chat. But good judgment prevailed.

Mr. Sabbatini grew up on the Lower
East Side and knew the city like a cab-
driver. He was also a Yankees fan, a
pleasant one. He had tickets, and we
rode the subway to the Bronx, to The
House That Ruth Built, and spent that
beautiful afternoon watching the Yankees, with Thurman Munson, Graig Net-
tles, and Bobby Murcer, play the Orioles, with Brooks Robinson, Boog
Powell, and Paul Blair.

Tom and I decided that we had been
narrow-minded in the selection of the
National League as our only potential
home. We discussed the possibility of
also playing for a team in the American
League. Mr. Sabbatini agreed that this
was wise on our part.

Something was different, though. My dreams were not as clear and exciting. My love for the game was not as deep. I joked along with Tom as we discussed which American League teams would be acceptable. We evaluated the important factors—uniform colors, stadium size, winning tradition, great players from the past, and so on—but it was not as much fun as it had been a month earlier.

Mr. Sabbatini listened and laughed and offered his advice. He was an exceptionally nice person, generous with his time and always kind with his comments. He seemed especially concerned about me. He understood the earthquakes and aftershocks that were rattling my world, and he wanted me to know that he was in my corner.

17

I walk into Wink's Waffles at 8:30 and ask for a table by the window. The place is full of seniors consuming far too many calories thanks to the latest coupon scheme devised to attract those over sixty-five. The hostess is reluctant to seat me where I want to be seated, so I inform her that I'm expecting at least three others. This works and I get my table, which, as I recall, is very near the one we had four years ago, when my girls met their paternal grandfather for the first and last time. I drink coffee, read the newspaper, and watch the parking lot.

At 8:55, a golf cart appears from the path next to the restaurant. It's Warren, alone. He parks in a row of other carts, stands slowly and stretches his back, then walks with the careful movements you would expect of a man who is recuperating from a nasty surgery. Sick as he is, there is still the unmistakable walk of an old man who was once a great athlete. Head high, chest up, a trace of a swagger. He's holding sheets of paper, no doubt my little memoir about his beanball.

I wave him over, and he joins me; no handshake, no smile. His eyes are red and puffy, as if sleep eluded him. He opens with a pleasant "You can't print this piece of shit."

"Well, good morning, Warren. Sleep well?"

"You heard me."

"I can and will, Warren. Why the crude language? Hit a bit too close to home? Surely you're not calling it a pack of lies?"

"It's a pack of lies."

The waitress appears, and he orders coffee. When she's gone, he says, "What are you trying to prove?"

"Nothing. What I'm trying to do is force you to face the consequences, for one of the few times in your life."

"Aren't you the wise one?"

"I'm not trying to be wise, Warren. You have a lot of unfinished business in your life, and this is one loose end you can wrap up before you're gone."

"I'm not going anywhere. I'm fighting this thing tooth and nail, and my doctors know a hell of a lot more than you do."

I am not going to argue about whether he is dying. If he thinks he is in the lucky 5 percent who will live for five years, I am in no position to say otherwise. His coffee arrives, and the waitress asks about the others who might be joining us.

"It's just the two of us," I say.

"Are you ready to order?"

"Sure. I guess I should have a waffle. Blueberry, with sausage."

"Nothing for me," he says gruffly, waving her away.

"Who do you think will print this crap?" he asks.

"Do you read *Sports Illustrated*?"

"No."

"There's a senior writer there named Jerry Kilpatrick. Baseball is his favorite beat. A Chicago guy, my age. I've talked to him twice, and he's interested in the story, and the truth. Joe Castle will never be forgotten in Chicago, and Kilpatrick thinks the story would be great. Especially after you're gone."

"You don't know the truth," he growls.

"We both know it, Warren."

He sips his coffee and gazes out the window. Finally, he says, "You have no idea what you're talking about. You don't know the game."

"Are you talking about the code, Warren? The little unwritten rules of baseball, one of which says that beanballs must be used to, number one, get guys off the plate, or, number two, retaliate when one of your players gets hit, or, number three, put a guy in his place if he shows up the pitcher. I can't remember numbers four and five. Is that what you're talking about, Warren? Because if it is, then you're dead wrong because Joe didn't crowd the plate, nobody was throwing at your hitters, and Joe did nothing to show you up. You wanted to hit him in the head because you envied his success, and you liked to hit players and start trouble, and, well, I don't know, Warren, what was your reason for the beanball? You used it so often. Maybe you realized you couldn't get him out, so you hit him in the head. Was that it, Warren?"

"You're clueless."

"Okay, then explain things to me, Warren. Why do you have no regrets about intentionally hitting Joe Castle in the face?"

"It's part of the game, sort of like the football player who breaks his neck or blows out a knee, never to play again. The boxer with brain damage. The race car driver who's killed in a crash. The skier who falls off a mountain. It's sports, okay? Bad things happen, and when they do, you don't run around crying and apologizing and trying to make everything okay. That's not the game as I knew it."

I will not bicker. I could blow holes in his twisted logic for the next hour and gain nothing. We take a break and listen to the chatter around us. Alone, the two of us, for the first time in decades. In fact, I can't remember the last time I was alone with my father. I've seen him half a dozen times since he abandoned us, and only a couple of those little meetings were his idea. There is so much I would like to say, none of it pleasant, and I battle the urge to unload a lifetime's worth of debris. But I promised myself I would not beat him up. Given his attitude at the moment, I doubt if Warren Tracey would sit still during a round of verbal abuse. He's still a fighter.

The waitress delivers the waffle, a thick dessert-like creation smothered in whipping cream. I take a bite of link sausage, something Sara would never consider buying, and dive back into our little session. "So, finally, after thirty years, you're admitting you deliberately hit Joe?"

"I'm really hesitant to say anything to you because you might add it to your little short story here. Since you're divulging family matters anyway, I don't trust you."

"Fair enough. You have my word that anything you say here today will not be included."

"Still don't trust you."

"I'm not going to argue such things as trust and responsibility, Warren. Why did you throw at Joe Castle?"

"He was a cocky kid, and I didn't like what he did to Dutch Patton. Dutch and I played together in Cleveland."

"He was not a cocky kid, no more so than any other major leaguer. And you did not play with Dutch Patton in Cleveland. Dutch never played for the Indians." I take a small bite of a large waffle, without taking my eyes off him. His mouth drops open and his eyes glow, as if he might throw a punch. Suddenly he grimaces and exhales as a jolt of pain shoots through his midsection. I forgot what he's going through.

"Are you okay?" I ask.

"I'm fine."

"You don't look fine."

"I'll be all right. I'm thinking about playing golf tomorrow."

I appreciate the change in subjects. We talk about golf for a few minutes, and the mood lightens considerably. Then it darkens again when I realize he has played golf since he was six years old; he won the Maryland Open when he was seventeen; and he has never played a single round with me. I understand the DNA thing, but the man across the table is nothing but my biological father. Nothing more.

I make quick work of the waffle and sausage and slide the platter away. "You were trying to explain why you beaned Joe. I don't think we finished that part of the conversation."

"You're so damned smart, why don't you explain it?" he snaps angrily.

"Oh, I know, Warren. I've known for a long time. There were several reasons you wanted to hit Joe, all twisted and pretty sick, but as you say, that was your game. You resented his success and the attention he was getting. In your warped mind, he showed you up after he hit his home run in the first inning. You wanted to be the first tough guy to hit him in the head. You loved hitting people and starting trouble. And you were envious because I, along with countless other little boys in the summer of 1973, worshipped Joe Castle. You had slapped me around. You were trying to make amends, trying to be my hero, and you couldn't stand the thought of me dreaming of becoming some other player. All of the above and probably more, but that's enough. I don't have access to your thoughts, thank God."

"So it was all about you?"

"I didn't say that, Warren. Only you know why you did it. The sick part is that you can't admit it. You've lied for thirty years and never had the spine to admit what you did." This sounds much harsher than I want it to be.

His shoulders sag a little, and there are tiny beads of sweat on his forehead. He pinches his nose and almost under his breath says, "I'm sorry I slapped you around, Paul."

I roll my eyes in frustration and want to curse. "You've apologized a hundred times for that, Warren. I'm not here because of the slapping. I'm not here to dredge up your deficiencies as a father. I buried those a long time ago."

With a paper napkin, he wipes the sweat from his face. His skin has lost what little color it had. He takes a sip of coffee and stares at me. In a voice that is suddenly weak and raspy, he says, "I threw at Joe, but I swear I didn't mean to hurt him."

I was waiting for this, one of baseball's greatest lies, one of the lamest excuses in the history of sports. I shake my head in disbelief and say, "Gee, what a surprise. The same asinine cop-out pitchers have been using for a hundred years. So, let me get this straight, Warren. You deliberately throw a fastball at a batter's face, at ninety or perhaps ninety-five miles an hour, from sixty feet away, a distance that gives him less than a second to react, with the intent, the goal, the dream to see the ball hit him somewhere above the neck and knock him to the ground, preferably in a state of unconsciousness. If they carry him off, no big deal. If he misses a few games, no big deal. Yet when the beanball actually does serious damage, you can hide behind the old faithful 'Gosh, I didn't mean to hurt him.' Can't you see how utterly ridiculous this is, Warren? You sound like a fool for saying it."

Again, I am aware that this sounds too harsh, but I'm fighting anger right now.

He drops his head, nods at something, then looks through the window. There is a crowd of seniors waiting around the front door. The hostess keeps looking our way. I think she wants our table, but I'm in no hurry.

He finally mumbles, "It was just part of the game."

"Your game, maybe," I shoot back. "But then, you were a headhunter."

"I was not."

"Then why did you throw at their heads? Why didn't you throw at Joe's thigh or hip or ribs, anything below the shoulder? That's what the code says, right, Warren? The code says sometimes you have to hit a guy—I understand that. But the code also says you never throw at a guy's head. But you were a tough guy, weren't you, Warren? You wanted to hit Joe in the head."

"I'm bored with this conversation. What do you want, Paul?"

"Let's take a trip together, go to Calico Rock. You can sit down with Joe and shake hands, say what you want to say, have a long chat about the game, about life, whatever. I'll be there. Joe has a couple of brothers who take care of him, I'm sure they'll be there. It will mean a lot to Joe and his family. I promise you, Warren, you will not regret doing this. Let's close this chapter. Now."

He picks up my story and says, "And if I don't, then you'll get this published after I'm gone?"

"That's the plan," I reply, doubting now that the blackmail was a good opening strategy.

Quickly, he rips it in two, tosses it at me, and says, "Go ahead. I'll be dead." He's on his feet and working his way through the crowd at the front door, moving nicely for an old sick man. He gets in the golf cart, grips the wheel, and pauses as if he's hit with another sharp pain. He gazes into the distance, waiting, deep in thought, and for a second I think that maybe he has changed his mind.

Then he drives away, and I am certain I will never see him again.

18

On September 23, the doctors released a statement about Joe's condition. Because of the trauma to the optic nerve, Joe had lost at least 80 percent of the vision in his right eye, and the loss was permanent. The probability of Joe playing again was, in their opinion, "extremely low."

The news broke the hearts of Cubs fans. Their annual "wait till next year" suddenly lost all of its promise and excitement. The greatest prospect in their long, frustrated history would never play again.

It also crushed the spirits of the players. Joe's teammates were struggling without him, and the news from New York was devastating. Later that afternoon they were blown out by the Braves, and they would lose the next three, falling two games behind the Mets, who were winning and on the verge of clinching the National League East. The Mets would go on to beat the Reds for the pennant, and do so without a player hitting over .300 or a pitcher winning twenty games. In the second coming of the Miracle Mets, they pushed the A's to seven games before losing the World Series.

The miraculous yet tragic career of Joe Castle came to an end. His numbers were mind-boggling—in thirty-eight games he had 160 at bats, seventy-eight hits, twenty-one home runs, twenty-one doubles, eight triples, thirty-one stolen bases, and forty-one RBIs. His batting average of .488 was the highest ever, but would not be entered into the record books because he didn't play enough. Other records would stand: (1) the first rookie to hit three home runs in his first game; (2) the first rookie to hit safely in his first nineteen games; (3) the first rookie to steal a base in nine consecutive games; (4) the first rookie to steal second and third in seven different games; and, his most famous, (5) fifteen consecutive hits in fifteen at bats. He tied several other rookie records, including four hits in his first game.

But on September 23, 1973, his numbers meant little to him and his fans.

———

My father eventually came home after being released by the Mets, and during the first family dinner he tried to appear upbeat about his future. Supposedly, several teams were interested in him for the 1974 season. Negotiations were under way, deals being offered. We listened and pretended to believe him, but we knew the truth.

In an effort to stay busy, he painted the inside of the garage, installed new gutters, worked on his car, and seemed to be making plans to live there for a long time.

My mother was playing a lot of tennis and secretly looking for a job.

I came home from school one afternoon and, as usual, planned to leave as soon as possible and hustle down the street to the Sabbatinis'. My father was in the den watching television, and when I walked through, he said, "Say, Paul, you got time for a catch? I need to keep my arm loose."

As bad as I wanted to say no, I couldn't do it. "Sure."

I had vowed to never again toss a baseball with my father.

———

. . . an open area where we had a small backstop and a wooden home plate. He grabbed me by the arm and said, "First of all, don't ever ignore me again like that. You hear me? I'm your father and I know a thousand times more baseball than those clowns who call themselves coaches." I tried to pull away, but he dug in with fingernails. He was getting angrier with each passing second. "You hear me? Don't ever ignore me again."

"Yes sir," I said, but only to keep from getting hit.

He let go and put his finger under my chin. "Look at me," he snarled. "Look me in the eyes when I'm talking to you. There's a right way and a wrong way to play this game, and you got it all wrong. Never, I repeat, never let a hitter show you up like that. At any level of the game, I don't care if you're eight years old or playing in the World Series, never let a hitter show you up like that. This is how you handle that type of an asshole. Get up there."

I took the bat and got in a stance at home plate. He backed away, maybe fifty feet. He was wearing his glove, and he had three baseballs in it. I was an eleven-year-old kid, without a batting helmet, facing a pitcher for the Mets, one who was not only angry but in the process of teaching me the crude art of hitting a batter.

"The code says he's getting hit, okay, so the next time he prances his cocky ass up to the plate, it's your job to hit him. Same as if one of your guys got plunked, then you gotta protect your team. Are you listening to me?"

"Yes sir."

"I do it with three pitches. Some guys go right at them and hit them with the first pitch. I don't do that, because most batters are looking for it on the first pitch. I set them up. My first pitch is a fastball a foot outside."

He took a windup and threw a fastball a foot outside. It wasn't full speed, but then I wasn't fully grown. The pitch looked awfully fast to me.

"Don't step out!" he growled. "Second pitch, same as the first." Another windup, another fastball a foot outside.

"Now, this is when you nail the son of a bitch. He's leaning in a little, thinking I'm picking at the outside corner, so he's not thinking about getting drilled. I'm not gonna hit you in the head, so don't step out, okay? Dig in, Paul, like a real player."

I was terrified and couldn't move.

He took his windup and threw the ball at me, not high and not as hard as he could, but when the ball hit my thigh, it hurt like hell and I think I screamed. He was yelling, "See. You're gonna survive. That's how you do it. Two fastballs away, then you hit the bastard, preferably in the head." He scurried around and picked up the three baseballs while I rubbed my thigh and tried not to cry. "Give me the bat and get your glove," he said.

I was now the pitcher, and he was at the plate. "Two fastballs outside. Let's go."

I delivered the first one in the grass and three feet off the plate. "You gotta hit the catcher's mitt, Paul, come on, damn it," he snarled as he waved the bat like a real hitter. His career batting average was .159.

I threw the second pitch outside and higher.

"Now," he said, taking a step toward me. "Drill me right here." He tapped the side of his head. "Stick it in my ear, Paul." He was back at the plate in his stance. "Stick it in my ear. You can't throw hard enough to hurt me."

I was forty feet away, gripping the baseball, wanting desperately to throw a pitch that would knock out his teeth, spill blood, fracture his skull, and lay him out flat on the grass. I kicked high, delivered, and the ball went straight down the middle of the plate, a perfect strike. As it bounced off the backstop, he picked it up, threw it back to me, and said, "Come on, you little chickenshit. Hit me with the damned baseball."

I threw another fastball, one that was higher but still over the plate. This made him even angrier, and after retrieving the ball, he fired it back. It was getting dark. He threw the ball much too hard. It glanced off the webbing of my glove and hit me in the chest. I shrieked and started crying, and before I realized it, he was in my face, yelling, "If you don't take this ball and hit me in the head, I'm gonna beat your ass, you understand?"

As he stomped to the plate, I glanced at the house. Upstairs, Jill was peeking out her bedroom window.

My third effort at beaning him was as unsuccessful as the first two. The pitch was high and inside, but not close enough to do the damage I wanted. To show his disgust, he reached out with his left hand and caught the pitch bare-handed. What an insult to a pitcher, but then I really didn't care. I just wanted to get away from this madman. He flung the bat toward the house and came after me.

"You're a coward, you know that, Paul? Nothing but a coward. It takes guts to throw at batters, but a pitcher has to do it."

"Not in Little League," I managed to say.

"In every league!"

I guess I was too small to punch, so he slapped me across the face with the back of his left hand, protecting, of course, his pitching hand. I screamed and fell down, and just as he grabbed me by the collar, I heard my mother yell, "Get away from him, Warren!"

She was standing ten feet away, holding the baseball bat, something she had probably never done before in her life, and aiming its barrel at my father. Jill was hiding behind her. For a few seconds no one moved, then, seeing the opportunity, I crawled away.

"Put the bat down," he said.

"You hit him in the face," she said. "What kind of animal are you?"

"He hit him with the baseball too," Jill added.

"Shut up," he snarled.

A few more seconds passed as everyone took a breath. We slowly made our way inside, each carefully watching the other. My parents went to the basement and fought for a long time, and when they got tired, he left.

(EXCERPT FROM "THE BEANING OF JOE CASTLE," BY PAUL TRACEY, SON OF WARREN)

19

Killing time in the Atlanta airport, I call Clarence Rook. It has been slightly more than twenty-four hours since I said good-bye to him, but it seems like a month. "You'll never guess who called me last night," he says.

"Charlie or Red?"

"Charlie. Said he got a call from Joe, who said I showed up at the field with a stranger, and he was just checking in to make sure everything's okay. That's what Charlie always says—'Clarence, everything okay?' I said, sure, Charlie,

just a nephew from Texas who wanted
to see the field."

"Why didn't you tell him the truth?" I
ask.

"Well, I did, later. I got to thinking
about it, chatted with Fay, and so I called
Charlie back, said I had something important to discuss with him and Red,
and could we meet for coffee? We did,
this morning, at a quieter place north of
town. I told them all about you, your
visit, and so on." He stops talking, and
this is not a good sign.

"Let me guess. They did not weep
with sorrow at the news that Warren
Tracey has terminal cancer."

"They did not."

A pause, another bad sign. "And the
idea of him coming to Calico Rock to
meet with Joe? How was that received?"

"Not very well, at least not at first. In
fact, they didn't like the idea of *you* being here."

"Will they shoot me if I return?"

"No. They warmed up considerably,
even promised to talk to Joe and see if
he likes the idea. I pushed a little, but

it's really none of my business. What about the meeting with your father?"

I decide to spin it. "I got the door open, I think. We had some frank discussions, a lot of old family stuff, nothing you want to hear. The problem is that he is in denial about his cancer, and until he faces the prospect of death, he will be hard to persuade."

"Poor guy."

"Maybe, but I could not reach the point where I actually felt sorry for him."

I ask about Fay, and the conversation runs out of gas. An hour later, I board the flight to Dallas.

Sara and the girls are waiting with a late dinner when I finally get home. The girls have no idea where I have been or what I've been doing, so we talk about the weekend we are about to spend camping in the mountains. Sara, though, is curious. After we're finished and the girls are gone, I replay the trip as we clear the table.

"What's next?" she asks.

"I have no idea. I might wait a couple of weeks and call Warren, ask about his chemo, maybe bring up Joe again."

"What's your favorite saying, dear? Didn't get halfway—"

"Didn't get halfway to first base. Yep, that pretty well sums up my little visit with Warren. He's still the tough guy, and he could take it to his grave. Probably will."

"Are you glad you went?"

"Yes, very much so. I got a glimpse of Joe Castle, and he's doing as well as possible, I guess. I got to see Warren, which doesn't mean much now but it could seem important one day. And, most important, I had a glass of Ozark peach brandy."

"What's that?"

"Moonshine."

"They serve it with dinner?"

"No, it's strictly an after-dinner drink, at least in the Rook household. Clarence called it a 'digestif.' "

"What does it taste like?"

"Liquid fire."

"Sounds delicious. Any other excitement?"

"Not really."

"Are you going to call Jill?"

"Not tonight, maybe later. I doubt if she wants to hear about Warren."

———

A week later, I leave the office for lunch and drive to a city-owned, multi-field complex where most of my friends have coached their sons in the various youth leagues. But for a few grounds-keepers, the place is empty. The season is over. I climb the bleachers of the "big field," as it is known, a regulation-size diamond with a center field wall four hundred feet away. I sit in the shade below the press box and eat a chicken wrap.

It is August 24, 2003. Thirty years ago tonight, I was sitting with my mother in Shea Stadium, watching my hero Joe Castle walk to the plate to face my father. I slowly recall those images and again hear the sound of Joe being struck. The horror, the chaos, the fear, the ambulance, then the fighting and the aftermath. His skull was cracked in three places. His cheekbone was broken. He was bleeding from his ears, and the doctors at first thought he was dead.

That time and place seem so far away now. The beanball ended two careers, and I'm not sure what it did to me. It broke the hearts of millions of people, so I wasn't the only one wounded. But I was the only one, aside from my parents, who knew Joe was about to get drilled in the head.

I wonder if Joe is marking the anniversary. Is he doing what I am doing—sitting alone in a ballpark, remembering the tragedy, and longing for what could have been? Somewhere in his altered state, does he look back with bitterness at what happened? I certainly would. Thirty years later, and I still get choked up thinking about the needless injury and the ending of a beautiful career.

I suspect this date means nothing to Warren Tracey. He is probably on the golf course. He dismissed the beanball decades ago. "It's sports. Bad things happen."

After lunch is finished, I sit and try to think of some way to put the story of Joe Castle behind me. I finally admit that I'm not sure that will ever happen.

Two weeks pass. The girls return to school, and I get lost in my work. Our normal, happy life resumes, and I slowly forget about the idea of a reunion in Calico Rock. The phone rings one night, and Rebecca, our ten-year-old, answers it. She runs into the den and says, "Dad, it's some man named Warren. Wants to talk to you."

Sara and I look at each other. Neither can remember the last time Warren called our home.

"Who's Warren?" Rebecca asks.

"Your grandfather," Sara says as I head to the kitchen.

The call has no purpose, as far as I can tell. His voice is scratchy and weak, and he informs me that chemotherapy is not pleasant. He has no appetite, so he's losing weight, along with his hair. Agnes drives him to the hospital twice a week for the infusions, which take two hours each in a depressing room with a dozen other cancer patients hooked up to their drips.

He stuns me by asking, "How's the

family?" And when Sara walks through the kitchen and hears me talking about our children, she is shocked. He informs me that he called Jill a few hours earlier, but no one answered the phone.

Warren Tracey is calling his children. He must be dying.

20

I check in with Clarence Rook once a week, but these conversations get shorter and shorter. There is not much news in Calico Rock, and I am not sure how he fills up a newspaper every Wednesday. I call Warren occasionally, not really out of a deep concern over his health, but more to remind him that I am still around and I want something. We never discuss Joe Castle.

In the second week of October, I am in the middle of a meeting with my boss and colleagues when my cell phone vibrates. At my company, it is not a crime

for a cell phone call to disrupt something important. I step into the hall and
say hello to Agnes. Warren is in the hospital, internal bleeding, low blood pressure, fainting spells. The doctors just
completed another scan, and the cancer has spread rapidly, tumors are everywhere—liver, kidneys, stomach, and,
worst of all, the brain. He has lost forty
pounds. She believes Warren is finally
accepting the fact that cancer will kill
him.

What am I supposed to say? I don't
know this woman, and I hardly know her
husband. I offer a few half-baked sym-
pathies and promise to call tomorrow. I
do, but go straight to voice mail. Three
days later, I am driving home from work
when Warren calls my cell. He says he
is back home, feels much better, has
changed doctors because the old ones
were idiots, and has a fighting chance
of beating his cancer. At the beginning
of the brief conversation, he sounds
alert, chipper, full of energy, but he cannot maintain the ruse. By the end, his
voice is fading, and his diction is not as
sharp. I go through my short list of things

to say, and I am ready to finish the call when he says, "Say, Paul, I've been thinking about that trip to Arkansas."

"Oh really," I say, avoiding any trace of excitement.

"Yes. I like the idea. Not sure my doctors will approve of me traveling, but let's give it a try."

"Sure, Warren. I'll make some calls."

———

The worst part will be the long drive, just me and Warren in the car, with so much history to cover and no desire to go there.

Our flights take us to Little Rock, and I arrive two hours before him. I eat lunch, kill time, work on my laptop, and find a spot to observe the arriving passengers. It's a small airport with lots of open spaces, natural light, and not too much traffic.

According to our last phone call, his doctors said no to the trip, and this only heightened his determination. He finally admitted the cancer is now in control of things, and he has stopped chemo. "I doubt if I'll make it to Christmas, Paul," he said, as if the holidays meant something to him.

Christmas. When I was eight, he was playing winter ball in Venezuela and was a no-show at Christmas. Jill and I opened gifts near the tree, and my mother could not stop crying. I wonder if Warren remembers all the things I remember.

He appears in a crowd with other passengers from Atlanta. He's wearing a cap because he has no hair, and he walks with a slow but determined step. He has shriveled into a small man with a girlish waistline and sunken chest. He's rolling a small carry-on behind him, and he's looking around for me.

I almost rented a hybrid for environmental reasons but realized we would be shoulder to shoulder for hours. Instead, we're in a large SUV with as much room as possible between the two front seats. Not much is said until Little Rock is behind us.

He has aged ten years in two months, and I understand why his doctors said no to the trip. He nods off repeatedly and for a long time says nothing, then really opens the door with "God, it's nice being away from Agnes."

I laugh and think of all the wild directions this conversation could now go. "What number is she—five or six?" I ask.

A pause as he calculates, then, "Agnes is number five. Karen was four. Florence was three. Daisy was two. Your mother was the first."

"Impressive that you can still remember the lineup."

"Oh, some things you never forget."

"Got a favorite?"

He thought about this for a while. We were on a two-lane road with farmland on both sides. "I never loved anyone like I loved your mother, at first anyway. But we were too young to get married. For love, it's your mother. For money, that would be Florence. For sex, Daisy gets the gold star."

"Sorry I asked."

"She was a stripper, Daisy. What a body."

"You left us for a stripper?"

"You wouldn't blame me if you saw her onstage."

"How long did it last?"

"Not long. I really can't remember. And I did not leave you for a stripper. The marriage was over when I happened to meet Daisy."

"In a strip club?"

"Of course. Where else does one meet a stripper?"

"Don't know. I have no experience in that area."

"Good for you."

"Were you ever faithful to Mom?"

Without hesitation, he says, "No."

"Why not?"

"I don't know," he says in frustration. "Why do men do anything? Why do they gamble away fortunes, or kill themselves with booze, or marry crazy women? I don't know. You drag me out here in the middle of Podunk, Arkansas, to ask why I chased women?"

"No, I did not. I don't really care now."

"How is your mother?"

"She's doing fine. I see her several

times a year. She's beautiful, as always."
I almost add that she's far better looking than Agnes but let it pass.

"Does she know I'm sick?"

"Yes, I told her back in August, as
soon as I heard about it."

"I doubt if she cares."

"Should she care, Warren?"

He takes a deep breath, then begins
to nod off. I silently urge him to fall
asleep, to take a long, two-hour nap.
His cancer is extremely painful, and
when he is awake, he seems uncomfortable. He keeps painkillers in his shirt
pocket.

We've touched briefly on his mar-
riages, one subject I had planned to
avoid. After he takes a nap, I hit pay dirt
with a simple question: "Did you ever
play baseball in Arkansas?"

"Oh yes, in the Texas League we
played the Arkansas Travelers several
times a year. A wonderful old stadium in
downtown Little Rock. Nice crowds."

The door swings wide open, and Warren springs to life. Forgotten games, old
teammates, strange happenings, locker

room humor, curfew violations, life in the bus leagues—we stay on the subject of minor-league baseball for a lot of miles. But he tires easily, and his long narratives stop suddenly when he needs water or a few moments with his eyes closed. He nods off again, things are quiet, then he's awake and remembering another story.

During his long, difficult career, he was stationed in dozens of small towns, some of which he has not thought about in years. They come back to him now, in a flood of memories. I am surprised to learn that Warren is a fine raconteur with a flair for the punch line. The more stories he tells, the more he remembers.

Why have I never heard these?

We do not talk about Joe Castle and the reason for this trip. I have no idea what Warren will say, but I have a hunch he does.

He coughs, grimaces, takes a pill, then nods off again. We are in the hills now, and it's getting dark.

On the edge of Mountain View, about an hour south of Calico Rock, I spot a nice, clean motel and pull in. I pay cash for two single rooms. Warren says he's not hungry and needs to lie down. I get a burger from a fast-food place and take it back to my room.

21

Clarence is waiting inside the front door of the *Calico Rock Record*. The morning is bright, the air light and cool, a far different feel from my last visit in August. Main Street is coming to life. We arrive at 9:00 a.m., as scheduled. Warren slept for ten hours and says he feels good.

"I'm very sorry about your illness, Mr. Tracey," Clarence says sincerely, after they shake hands.

"Thank you. And it's Warren, okay?"

"Sure. Would you like some coffee?"

We would, and we gather in Clarence's wonderfully cluttered office for the morning ritual of coffee. Clarence brings us up to speed on the latest conversations with the Castle clan. They have yet to agree to a meeting, but they haven't ruled one out either. Clarence thinks things will go well if we simply show up. I knew before I left Santa Fe, and Warren knew before he left Florida, that such a meeting might not take place, but we agreed to try anyway. On the phone, Warren said he would feel better having tried to speak with Joe, if indeed Joe has no desire to meet.

We ride with Clarence across town to the high school. Again, Joe is on his red Toro mower, slowly and meticulously riding back and forth across the outfield, cutting grass that is no longer growing. It is October and the grass is turning brown. Near the third base dugout, we climb the bleachers and take a seat. Two middle-aged men are sitting in the first base dugout. "Red and Charlie," Clarence says as we settle into our places with nothing to do but watch Joe cut grass. There is no one else around. It's almost 10:00 a.m., and the high school is busy in the distance.

"And he does this every day?" Warren asks. He's to my left, Clarence to
my right.

"Five days a week if the weather is
nice," Clarence says. "March through
November."

"It's a beautiful field," Warren says.

"They give an award each year for the
best high school baseball field in the
state. We've won it so many times I can't
keep up. I guess it helps when you have
a full-time groundskeeper."

After a few more surgical cuts, Joe
lifts his blades and heads for the first
base dugout. He kills the engine, gets
off the mower, and says something to
his brothers. One of them steps out of
the dugout with two folding chairs that
he carries to a spot just in front of home
plate. "That's Red," Clarence says quietly.

Red unfolds the chairs, arranges them
so that they are facing the pitcher's
mound, and when their placement suits
him, he takes a few steps in our direction, stops, and says, "Mr. Tracey."

"I think that's you," I say to Warren,
who gets to his feet and slowly makes

his way down the bleachers to the field. He is met by Red, who extends a hand and says, "I'm Red Castle. Nice to meet you."

They shake hands and Warren says, "Thanks for doing this."

Joe is shuffling toward the chairs, his cane poking the ground in front of him, his feet doing their sad little stutter steps. His left arm and hand hang by his side, and he works the cane with his right hand. When he is close enough, he stops and offers it. Warren takes it with both of his hands, grasps it, and says, "It's good to see you, Joe."

When Joe speaks, it is in a high-pitched, halting staccato, as if he knows precisely what the next word will be but getting it out requires some effort. "Thanks . . . for . . . coming." They sit in the chairs at home plate, and Red goes back to the first base dugout.

With their shoulders almost touching, they sit for a moment and stare out beyond the mound, their thoughts known only to themselves.

"You have a beautiful field here, Joe."

"Thanks."

From where we sit, we cannot hear them. Red and Charlie are seated on the bench in the dugout, likewise too far away to hear.

"A long way from Shea Stadium," Clarence says softly.

"A thousand miles and a thousand years. Thanks for doing this."

"You did it, Paul, not me. I'm happy to be in the middle of it—a reporter's dream. How many die-hard baseball fans in this country would kill to have our seats right now?"

I shake my head. "A couple of million in Chicago alone."

———

Joe says, "Sorry . . . about . . . the . . . cancer."

"Thanks, Joe. Just a bad break, you know. Bad luck. Sometimes you get lucky; sometimes you don't."

Joe nods. He is acquainted with bad luck. A minute passes as they sit and stare and ponder what to say next.

"I think we're supposed to talk about

baseball, Joe. That's the reason I'm here."

Joe is still nodding. "Okay."

"How often do you think about that night at Shea Stadium, Joe, the last time we saw each other?"

"Not . . . much . . . Don't . . . remember . . . much."

"Well, I'm envious, because I remember too well. It was a beanball, Joe, one I threw at your head as hard as I could possibly throw a baseball. I wanted to hit you, to knock you down, to put you in your place, and all that crap. It was intentional, Joe, and I've regretted it ever since. I'm sorry. I apologize. It was a nasty, mean-spirited, really stupid thing to do, and it ruined what was destined to be a great career. There—I said it. I'm sorry, Joe."

Joe nods and nods and finally says, "It's . . . okay . . . it's . . . okay."

Warren is on a roll and wants to unload everything. "I meant to hit you, Joe, but I had no idea all the bad stuff would happen. I know that sounds crazy. You throw a fastball at a guy's head with the clear intention of hitting him, yet you say you didn't really mean to hurt him. It's foolish, I know. So I guess I was a fool as well as an idiot."

"It's . . . okay . . . it's . . . okay."

"When I let it go, I knew it was on-target. I knew it would land somewhere above the neck. But it was too perfect, and for a split second you didn't move. When it hit, I could hear bones break. A lot of people heard bones break that night. It was pretty scary. I knew you were hurt. When they put you on the stretcher, I thought you were dead. God, I'm sorry, Joe."

"It's . . . okay . . . Warren."

There was a long gap in the conversation as both men continued to gaze into the distance. Warren says, "Do you remember your first at bat that night, the home run?"

"I . . . remember . . . every . . . home . . . run."

Warren smiles. Typical hitter. "At one point, you fouled off eight straight pitches. I had never seen a bat that quick. I threw fastballs, sliders, curves, changeups, even a cutter, and you just waited and waited until the last possible split second, then flicked the bat and fouled them off. The home run you hit was four inches off the plate. I fooled you all right, but you recovered and hit it almost four hundred feet. That's when I decided to hit you. I was thinking, well, if I can't get him out, I'll just knock him down. Intimidate him. He's just a rookie."

"Just . . . part . . . of . . . the . . . game."

"Maybe. A lot of players have been hit in the head, but few got hurt. Ray Chapman was killed by a pitch in 1920. Mickey Cochrane never played again after taking one in the head. Tony Conigliaro was a certain Hall of Famer, then he got beaned in the eye. I hit him once, did you know that?"

"Tony C.?"

"Yep. In 1965, I was pitching for Cleveland. Tony crowded the plate, and he was fearless. I drilled him in the shoulder and never felt bad about it. Sometimes you gotta hit a guy, Joe, you know that. But you don't try to hurt someone; it's never part of the game to throw at a guy's head. He's got a family, a career. That was my mistake."

"You . . . hit . . . a . . . lot . . . of . . . people."

Warren takes a deep breath and re-adjusts his weight. He took a pain pill an hour earlier, and it's wearing off. "True, and I have a lot of regrets, Joe. When I die, they won't say anything about what a lousy husband and father I was. They won't say much about my mediocre baseball career. No. What they'll write about is that one pitch. I threw a million, but they'll talk about the beanball that nailed Joe Castle. The one I'll always re-gret."

"Me . . . too."

Both men find this funny and begin laughing softly.

"You have every right to hate me, Joe. I cost you so much. In the blink of an eye, your career was gone, and there was no one to blame but me. It would be nice, as I'm getting close to the end, to know that you don't hate me. Is this asking too much?"

"I . . . hate . . . no . . . one."

"Even me? Come on, Joe, surely you've had some really evil thoughts about me over the years."

"I . . . did . . . but . . . not . . . now . . . You . . . said . . . it . . . was . . . an . . . accident . . . and . . . I . . . wanted . . . to . . . believe . . . you."

"But I was lying, Joe. It wasn't an accident. I lied about it for thirty years. Now I'm telling you the truth. Does this make you hate me?"

"No . . . You . . . apologized . . . I . . . accept."

Warren puts his right hand on Joe's left shoulder and says, "Thank you, Joe. You're a much bigger man than me."

"I'm . . . still . . . batting . . . a . . . thousand . . . off . . . you."

Warren laughs loudly, and Joe follows.

————

We watch and are amused at their ability to laugh. I've known my entire life that Warren Tracey has no sense of humor, so it's obvious Joe has said something funny.

"I think they're getting along," Clarence observes.

"I suppose they have to. If a fight breaks out, Warren has no one in his corner."

"They're in no mood for a fight. Charlie told me yesterday they admired your father for wanting to see Joe."

"What was their hesitation?"

"Two reasons. They were afraid it might upset Joe and bring back a lot of bad memories. And they're afraid this little meeting might somehow get leaked and end up in a story somewhere. I assured them that would not happen. Right?"

"Of course."

"So how did you blackmail your father into coming?"

"The blackmail didn't work. He's here because he wants to be here. He's a tough guy, and it's taken the reality of death to soften him up. He's looking back at a sloppy life with a lot of regrets."

"What an awful way to die."

"Yes, I'm sure it is."

Joe looks at the first base dugout and says, "Charlie . . . Red." His brothers get to their feet and leave the dugout.

Warren stands, looks at us, and waves us down.

We meet in front of home plate, and I shake hands with Joe Castle. He wears a cap, and thick, dark sunglasses to cover his bad eye. His hair is half gray, and he looks nothing like the smiling kid on the magazine covers of thirty years ago. In all fairness, though, who does look the same after thirty years?

Charlie and Red are nice enough but would rather observe than participate.

At my request, Clarence has a camera, and I explain to the Castles that I would like some photos to record the meeting. "Will they be published?" Red asks.

"Only with your approval," I say. He and Charlie are suspicious, but they agree.

To my surprise, Clarence has brought something else. From a small plastic bag kept somewhere inside his coat, he pulls out two baseball caps—Cubs and Mets. He hands them to Joe and Warren and says, "I thought it would be a nice touch to photograph you guys in these."

Joe looks at his with a frown, and Warren does the same. They are hesitant, as if the caps bring back too many memories. "Just a thought," Clarence says, retreating, as if he might have screwed up the entire meeting. Then Joe creases the bill of his cap, removes the one advertising a feed store, and puts on his Cubs cap. Like all ballplayers, he adjusts here and there until it feels right. When Warren removes his golf cap, his head is as slick as an onion, not a single hair, and for a split second we recoil at the horrors of chemotherapy. It is a reminder that he doesn't have long.

With the caps in place, we take a step back and Clarence snaps away. The two players are standing, smiling, with Joe leaning on his cane. Clarence has a better idea. He suggests we move to right center and use the scoreboard of Joe Castle Field as a backdrop. This we do, and after a few dozen shots of Joe and Warren, I wedge myself into the frame and stand between my father and my old hero, all smiling.

The eight-by-ten will be the final entry in my Joe Castle scrapbook.

Suddenly there is nothing left to do. The two have met, said what needed to be said, and posed for photos. We say our good-byes and leave the field.

Driving back to Main Street, Clarence says that Fay would like to have an early lunch on the porch, if that's okay. I glance at Warren in the rear seat, and he is shaking his head no. I do not want to offend Fay, or Clarence, so I say, "That's nice, but we need to hit the road. Warren has a 4:00 p.m. flight." I don't feel bad about this, because I've seen enough of Calico Rock. And, being so hospitable, the Rooks would love nothing more than to spend the entire afternoon on the porch swapping stories and taking more photos. Then the lemon gins.

"No problem," Clarence says. He

parks and we meet at his rear bumper. I thank him again, and he offers his best wishes to Warren. I promise to call with updates.

Not far out of Calico Rock, Warren, who has gone silent, asks me to pull over. He gets into the backseat and falls asleep. The trip and the meeting with Joe have exhausted him, and he's finally hit the wall.

He is still wearing his Mets cap.

22

According to the radar map, the weather from Santa Fe all the way east through Little Rock and down to Florida is perfectly clear. Yet both of our flights are delayed. Warren is fading fast, and I want him on a plane back to Agnes before there is an emergency I don't care to deal with. The delays have crowded the Little Rock airport, and we pass a few hours doing the mundane things passengers do while waiting.

Throughout the afternoon, when he was awake and felt like talking, our conversations were light. He never men-

tioned Joe. Though I have not been
around him enough to gauge his moods
or thoughts, it is obvious that his wheels
are turning. I am sure the subject of
death is paramount, as it would be for
anyone in his condition. I am sure he
has regrets, but neither of us wants to
go there. Warren cannot begin to repair
our troubled history with a few eleventh-
hour apologies, and we both understand
this. I am not sure he wants to try, but I
am certain I do not want to hear it.

His appetite comes and goes, and
when he says, "I'm hungry," we find a
small table in a crowded airport lounge.
When the waitress asks if we want
something to drink, Warren smiles and
says, "Yes, I want a tall mug of draft
beer." I order the same, and when she's
gone, he says, "I've been sober for ten
years. With two months to go, why
not?"

"Why not?"

"Sobriety is overrated, Paul," he says
with a grin. "I was much happier when I
was drinking."

I cannot smile along with this because

I remember him hitting my mother when he was drunk. "I wouldn't know," I say.

The bar has three large televisions, all tuned in to the World Series, Yankees versus Marlins. The beer arrives, we tap glasses, say cheers, and take sips. He savors his as if he were dying of thirst. He smacks his lips and says, "Oh, how I've missed this."

We order sandwiches and watch the game. It doesn't take long for him to disapprove. "Look at these guys," he snarls. "Look at how fat they are, especially the pitchers." A minute later, "Look at that guy, in the World Series, making millions a year, and he can't run out a pop fly."

Once again, I am struck by the absurdity of what I'm doing. Having a beer and watching a baseball game with my father—for the first time in my life! And only because he is now dying.

The food arrives, and we turn our attention away from the game. He has made a few derogatory comments about "these modern ballplayers," and I gather that Warren is not much of a fan.

"So, are you planning another story,

one about this little trip of ours?" he asks as he bites into a turkey club.

"No, I have no plans."

"I think you should. I think you should take the first story, add the second chapter, and get it printed. And do it now, before I die. I don't care. You want the world to know the truth, so do I. Publish it."

"That was not the deal, Warren."

"Who cares about the deal? I kinda like the idea of people knowing I went to see Joe Castle and after all these years I said I was sorry. I haven't done that too many times in my life."

"I'm sure you haven't."

"Publish it. I don't care."

"I couldn't do it without the approval of the Castles. You saw how protective they are."

"Then get their approval. Write it, show it to them, and I'll bet you can convince them."

"We'll talk about it." The idea is intriguing. We order another round and finish eating. A guy walks by and says, "The Mets suck," and keeps walking. We realize it's the cap and laugh.

One delay leads to another, and it's almost 9:00 p.m. when Warren's flight is called. His gate is near mine, and we walk slowly along the corridor. They are boarding when we arrive.

He takes a deep breath and looks me in the eyes. "Listen, thanks for doing this. It means a lot to me, and it meant a lot to Joe. A real burden has been lifted."

"It's known as the restorative powers of forgiveness."

"Aren't you the wiseass?"

"I suppose."

"It's true, Paul, you're a lot wiser than me because you'll live a life with few regrets. Me, I'll die with a long list of things I'd like to do differently. This is not a pleasant way to go."

"You can't fix it now, Warren."

He offers a hand, and we shake. "You're right. But I have a lot of regrets, Paul."

I have no response to this. I cannot offer a shallow and meaningless "Oh, it's okay, Warren, all is forgiven." We shake hands again, and it's obvious he wants a quick embrace. I do not.

He turns and drifts away and never looks back.

23

Agnes calls every other day with the latest on his deteriorating condition. He's
stopped eating; his systems are shut-
ting down; he's in the hospital; he's back
home; he's been turned over to hospice.
Warren is behaving like the Warren of
old—unable to place the calls himself,
unwilling to talk. Sara asks me repeatedly if I want to go see him.

No. I have already seen him.

Jill and I chat occasionally. It's the
Tracey family at its finest—Warren talks
to Agnes, who calls me, and I call my
sister. Jill does not want to talk to him,

to see him, or to show up at a memorial service after he is gone.

He lingers, and the calls from Agnes become monotonous. I look at the calendar. Thanksgiving is approaching, and I hope Warren does not upset our plans.

He does not. He dies on November 10, at the age of sixty-five, alone in a hospice facility. Agnes tells me that a memorial service is planned for Friday of the following week. Sara and I have a somewhat testy and prolonged disagreement about whether she should attend the service with me. I am adamant that she is not going; she feels some sort of weird obligation to pay her respects to a man she hardly knew, a man who skipped our wedding and offered not a single word of congratulations when our three girls were born. There is no family to sit with and mourn. There will be no post-burial get-together.

Sara has no business going. Besides, I don't want to blow another $500 on a plane ticket. When the discussion is over, she grudgingly concedes.

A lot of people die in Florida, and many are retirees without deep roots in their communities. Because of this, the burial business is efficient and stream-lined. The services tend to be small, quick, even impersonal.

Warren wanted to be cremated, and his wishes are carried out. His memorial is held in the windowless chapel of a mausoleum not far from his home. With perfect timing, I arrive, alone, fifteen minutes before the service and find Agnes sitting in the family's private waiting room. Some family. It's Agnes and her daughter, Lydia, a person I've never met, and me. You would think that a man who married five women would gener-ate a bit more interest.

We sit and talk, and the clock abso-lutely stops. Agnes again asks me if I want to give a eulogy or say a few words. Again, I politely decline, and use the ex-cuse that I might not be able to control my emotions and do not want to em-barrass myself. Emotions aside, any warm and touching thoughts or stories I could add at this point would be out-right fabrications.

Lydia, who eyes me suspiciously, finally gets down to business. "You know, Paul, we've already read his last will and testament."

I throw up both hands and say, "I don't care what's in it. I want nothing. I will accept nothing. If my name is mentioned, I will refuse to take anything."

"He left you and Jill $10,000 each," Agnes says.

Dividing the spoils before the burial seems in bad taste, but I let it pass. "I can't speak for Jill," I say, "but I don't want it. He never gave me a dime when I was in high school or college or when I needed a little extra, and I'm not taking his money now."

"I guess that's between you and the lawyers," Lydia says, and I get the impression she has had some experience with lawyers.

"I guess so."

"And he left $25,000 to a baseball field in Calico Rock, Arkansas," Agnes says.

This actually makes me smile, and I say, "That's nice." Good for Warren.

I am not going to ask about the size of the estate—the timing is bad, and I don't really care, and I'll find out later during probate.

We move next door to the chapel. There are about twenty seniors standing around the front pew, whispering, waiting, all in fine spirits it seems. The attire is Florida geezer casual—a lot of sandals and not a single jacket or tie. I avoid introducing myself to these people. I will never see them again, and I'm not about to swap a story or two about how great my old man was. I assume they are neighbors, golfing buddies, or Agnes's friends. I also assume that none of the men played professional baseball and shared a locker room with Warren Tracey. I know for a fact that there are no members of the 1973 Mets.

The chapel has dark stone walls and feels like a dungeon. An appropriate, mournful hymn is being piped in. A man in a suit asks us to please be seated. Thankfully, there is no reserved pew for the family. I ease away, toward the rear. Agnes has yet to shed a tear, and I suspect she will not be the only one to make it through with dry eyes. The friends and family sit and wait and absorb the mood music.

I don't know why I am here. Warren is gone, and if he could watch, he would not give a damn if I showed up or not. The notion of properly paying one's respects is ludicrous. The dead person could not care less. He is lying up there in a casket or, in Warren's case, a small blue urn next to the podium.

What did Yogi Berra say? "Always go to other people's funerals, otherwise they won't go to yours."

A guy in a black robe appears, probably of the generic dial-a-priest variety because Warren Tracey never went near a church. Maybe Agnes belongs to one. The priest chats with her, soothes her, then steps up to the small podium, spreads his arms like Charlton Heston at the Red Sea, and says, "Welcome."

The rear door opens quietly and catches my attention. Three men enter the chapel—Red Castle, then Joe with his cane and jerky gait, then Charlie.

They ease into the rear pew without making a sound. All three are wearing navy blazers and white shirts, by far the best dressed of anyone here.

I am shocked, and then I am not. What a brilliant, classy thing to do.

Instinctively, I get up and walk back to where they are sitting. I ease into the pew in front of them and whisper to Red, "Thanks for coming." All three nod. "What are you doing here?" I ask.

Charlie points to Joe and says, "Joe wanted to take a road trip."

"Welcome," the priest says louder, in our direction. I look at him, and he seems ready to rap our knuckles for talking during his sermon. I stay where I am, with the Castle boys, and we endure a meaningless ritual that is painfully stretched into thirty minutes. The highlight is a eulogy by Marv somebody from, of course, the golf club. Marv tells a real knee-slapper about playing golf with Warren one day. Warren was driving the golf cart. His ball was in the water. He got too close to the edge of the pond, flipped the cart, Marv almost drowned, and Warren avoided getting splashed with a single drop of water.

We laugh because we are expected to. Marv's not much of a speaker, and I get the impression he drew the short straw. I can just see these old goats sitting around the men's grill, playing gin rummy, arguing about who will speak at whose funeral. "Okay, Marv, you do Warren, and I'll do yours, and Fred'll do mine."

The priest does a credible job of filling in the gaps. He reads some scripture, relying heavily on the book of Psalms. He hits the high points of God's love, goodness, forgiveness, salvation, and it becomes obvious that whatever Agnes is, she is not Catholic, Jewish, or Muslim. He never mentions the fact that Warren played professional baseball. Winding down, he informs us that Warren will be interred down the hall, on Wall D of the Third Pavilion, but that this will be done privately, family only.

I decide to skip this. I have no desire to see the hole in the wall where Warren's ashes will spend eternity. Agnes can handle it. She's the only one who might stop by once a month for the next three months, touch his name in stone, and try to conjure up some emotion. I know I'll never be back.

Besides, I want to talk to Joe.

24

The Meditation Room is empty, and we claim it for the next few minutes. It's even more of a dungeon than the chapel and gives the appearance of never being used. We move four chairs into a circle and have a seat.

"I'm very touched that you guys would drive this far," I begin.

Red says, "Joe hasn't been to Florida since spring training of 1973. He wanted to get out of town, and so here we are." I remind myself that all three played minor-league ball, and like most prospects they arrived in camp each spring just like the veterans. Moving up and down the ranks of the minors and riding the buses, they have seen more of the country than I have.

"Thank you for coming," I say.

Charlie says, "And thank you for bringing your dad to Calico Rock. It meant more to Joe than you'll ever know." Joe is smiling, nodding, content to allow his brothers to do most of the talking.

Red adds, "It really meant a lot."

Joe says, "Sorry . . . about . . . your . . . dad."

"Thank you, Joe." He's still wearing the sunglasses to hide his bad eye, but just above them a slight indentation is visible at the corner of his forehead. They said he stopped breathing three times on the way to the hospital.

Red says, "Joe has something for you."

With his good hand, Joe reaches into the inside pocket of his blazer and pulls out an envelope. Though I have not seen it in thirty years, I recognize it immediately. It is the letter I left on the Joe Castle Wall at Mount Sinai Hospital, in September 1973. Joe hands it to me

with a wide smile and says, "Here . . .
I . . . want . . . you . . . to . . . have . . .
it."

I slowly open it and remove my letter.
I absorb the carefully printed heartache
of an eleven-year-old boy: "Dear Joe:
I am Paul Tracey, Warren's son. I am so
sorry for what my father did." As I read
on, I am overcome with the emotions
that ran so deep that summer and fall.
For six weeks, Joe Castle was my world.
I thought about him constantly. I read
everything I could find about him. I followed every one of his games, knew all
his statistics. I even dreamed of playing
on the same team with Joe—he was
only ten years older. If I broke in at
twenty, he would still be in his prime.
We could be teammates.

Then he was hurt. Then he was gone.
Then he was history.

When I finish the letter, my eyes are
moist, but I am determined to collect
myself. "Thanks, Joe."

Red says, "The Cubs did a nice job of
collecting all of Joe's stuff, including
several boxes of letters and gifts left at
the hospital. A few months after Joe

came home, they shipped it all down, and it's been in Mom's attic ever since."

Charlie takes over. "Six thousand letters from the hospital alone, over thirty thousand total. A couple of years later, Joe was going through the letters and came across yours. He put it in a special place."

Joe says, "It's . . . very . . . special."

"Thank you, Joe." I feel myself getting choked up again.

After a long silence, Red changes subjects. "Mr. Rook down at the newspaper said something about a story you were writing, a story about your dad and Joe. Is this true?"

"Sort of. I've written one story, but don't worry. I'm not going to publish it."

Charlie says, "Why not? Why don't you write a story about bringing your dad to Calico Rock, meeting Joe, telling the truth about what happened? You could even use one of the photos of Joe and Warren with their team caps on."

Joe is smiling and says, "I . . . would . . . like . . . that."

Charlie continues, "We might want to look at it first, you know, just to be safe, but we've kicked it around, and we think there are a lot of baseball fans out there who would enjoy the story. You know, Joe still gets letters."

I'm not sure how to respond. Warren wanted me to finish the story and get it published. Now Joe does too. "Give me some time to think about it," I say.

"Would it be a book?" Red asks.

"I don't think so. Probably a long magazine piece."

"Well, for what it's worth, we like the idea."

"Good. I'll give it some thought."

"Mr. Rook likes the idea too," Charlie says.

Clarence and I have discussed the idea on two occasions. I think he secretly wants to write the story himself, but he cannot bring himself to say so.

We chat for a few minutes. They are curious about me and my family, my mother and sister, and what happened to us after Warren was gone. When I mention that I am a graduate of the University of Oklahoma, this is instantly met with disapproval. They are die-hard Razorback fans, and of course their team is superior. We banter back and forth with the football chatter that sustains so many conversations in November.

The Meditation Room is suddenly in demand. Some mourners arrive and we leave. There is no sign of Agnes, Marv, the priest, or anyone else who said good-bye to Warren, and we make our way out of the mausoleum. The brothers are headed to Key West, for two days of deep-sea fishing, something Joe has wanted to do for years.

We shake hands and say good-bye in the parking lot. I watch them load into a late-model pickup truck with a club cab and a Razorback bumper sticker. I wave as they drive away.

Two hours later, I'm on the plane headed home. I read my letter and again feel the pain of a broken little boy. I put it away, open my laptop, and begin writing the story of Calico Joe.

Author's Note

The mixing of real people, places, and events into a novel is tricky business. This is a story about the Cubs and Mets and the 1973 season, but, please, all you die-hard fans, don't read this with any expectation of accuracy. I have completely rearranged schedules, rosters, rotations, records, batting orders, and I've even thrown in some fictional players to mix it up with the real ones. This is a novel, so any mistake should be promptly classified as part of the fiction.

Allow me to thank a few folks. Don

Kessinger is an old buddy from the Oxford days. He read the first draft of *Calico Joe* and found a few areas in need of more work. He was the Cubs shortstop from 1964 to 1975 and can hold his own with any big-league raconteur. Don later managed the White Sox, and he was replaced in 1979 by Tony LaRussa, who made his final appearance as a player for the Cubs in 1973 (before the arrival of Joe Castle) and who wore (briefly) Number 42 (Joe's first number). One of Tony's favorite dinner topics is baseball's "code," and, more specifically, the ins and outs of protecting one's teammates, and retaliation, and the complications of "throwing inside."

Thanks also to David Gernert, Alan Swanson, Talmage Boston, Michael Harvey, Bill MacIlwaine, Gail Robinson, and Erik Allen.

John Grisham
December 1, 2011